BACK TO BANK STREET

BY:
BROOKE ST. JAMES

Published in Nashville, Tennessee, by Elm Hill, an imprint of Thomas Nelson. Elm Hill and Thomas Nelson are registered trademarks of HarperCollins Christian Publishing, Inc.

Elm Hill titles may be purchased in bulk for educational, business, fund-raising, or sales promotional use. For information, please e-mail SpecialMarkets@ThomasNelson.com.

ISBN 978-1-4003-4091-0

Other titles available from Brooke St. James:

Another Shot:
(A Modern-Day Ruth and Boaz Story)

When Lightning Strikes

Something of a Storm (All in Good Time #1)
Someone Someday (All in Good Time #2)

Finally My Forever (Meant for Me #1)
Finally My Heart's Desire (Meant for Me #2)
Finally My Happy Ending (Meant for Me #3)

Shot by Cupid's Arrow

Dreams of Us

Meet Me in Myrtle Beach (Hunt Family #1)
Kiss Me in Carolina (Hunt Family #2)
California's Calling (Hunt Family #3)
Back to the Beach (Hunt Family #4)
It's About Time (Hunt Family #5)

Loved Bayou (Martin Family #1)
Dear California (Martin Family #2)
My One Regret (Martin Family #3)
Broken and Beautiful (Martin Family #4)
Back to the Bayou (Martin Family #5)

Almost Christmas

JFK to Dublin (Shower & Shelter Artist Collective #1)
Not Your Average Joe (Shower & Shelter Artist Collective #2)
So Much for Boundaries (Shower & Shelter Artist Collective #3)
Suddenly Starstruck (Shower & Shelter Artist Collective #4)
Love Stung (Shower & Shelter Artist Collective #5)
My American Angel (Shower & Shelter Artist Collective #6)

Summer of '65 (Bishop Family #1)
Jesse's Girl (Bishop Family #2)
Maybe Memphis (Bishop Family #3)
So Happy Together (Bishop Family #4)
My Little Gypsy (Bishop Family #5)
Malibu by Moonlight (Bishop Family #6)
The Harder They Fall (Bishop Family #7)
Come Friday (Bishop Family #8)
Something Lovely (Bishop Family #9)

So This is Love (Miami Stories #1)
All In (Miami Stories #2)
Something Precious (Miami Stories #3)

The Suite Life (The Family Stone #1)
Feels Like Forever (The Family Stone #2)
Treat You Better (The Family Stone #3)
The Sweetheart of Summer Street (The Family Stone #4)
Out of Nowhere (The Family Stone #5)

Delicate Balance (Blair Brothers #1)
Cherished (Blair Brothers #2)
The Whole Story (Blair Brothers #3)
Dream Chaser (Blair Brothers #4)

Kiss & Tell (Novella) (Tanner Family #0)
Mischief & Mayhem (Tanner Family #1
Reckless & Wild (Tanner Family #2)
Heart & Soul (Tanner Family #3)
Me & Mister Everything (Tanner Family #4)
Through & Through (Tanner Family #5)
Lost & Found (Tanner Family #6)
Sparks & Embers (Tanner Family #7)
Young & Wild (Tanner Family #8)

Easy Does It (Bank Street Stories #1)
The Trouble with Crushes (Bank Street Stories #2)
A King for Christmas (Novella) (A Bank Street Christmas)
Diamonds Are Forever (Bank Street Stories #3)
Secret Rooms and Stolen Kisses (Bank Street Stories #4)
Feels Like Home (Bank Street Stories #5)
Just Like Romeo and Juliet (Bank Street Stories #6)
See You in Seattle (Bank Street Stories #7)
The Sweetest Thing (Bank Street Stories #8)
Back to Bank Street (Bank Street Stories #9)

Split Decision (How to Tame a Heartbreaker #1)
B-Side (How to Tame a Heartbreaker #2)

Cole for Christmas

Somewhere in Seattle (Alexander Family #1)
Wildest Dream (Alexander Family #2)
About to Fall (Alexander Family #3)

Hope for the Best (Morgan Family #1)
Full Circle (Morgan Family #2)
Just for Tonight (Morgan Family #3)
Way Past Mistletoe (Morgan Family #4)
The Wild One (Morgan Family #5)

TABLE OF CONTENTS

TABLE OF CONTENTS

CHAPTER 1

Mid-December
Galveston, Texas

Ozzy Abramson, oldest son of Sean and Jenny Abramson,
grandson of James and Laney Graham.

Ozzy

*H*is mother, Jenny, came from a prominent family in
Galveston. She was popular in school. She was a
cheerleader and she hung out with the in-crowd, but she had
a side group of friends that most of the adults in her life didn't
approve of. Jenny was a free spirit—a rock-n-roller. She was a
twin, and her brother, Josh, was as straight-laced as they came.
But Jenny was a wild one.

She married a good man named Sean who kept her in line
(mostly). She did talk him into naming all three of their sons
after rockstars—Ozzy, their oldest, for Ozzy Osbourne, of

1

course. Their younger two boys were twins, like their mother. The older twin was named David for David Bowie, and the younger was Alec for Alec Stone. All three of Jenny's boys grew up to be art and music lovers like their mom.

They were all part of a large, close-knit family that was chock-full of professional athletes. Jenny's boys played some soccer growing up, but they lived in Texas where football was king, and none of them had been football/baseball type of boys.

Billy Castro, the famous boxer, was also tied to their family, and Jenny's boys didn't do much boxing. So, Ozzy, David, and Alec had always come across as *the artsy ones* even though they were all decent soccer players.

Jenny had aunts, uncles, and lots of cousins, and her boys grew up going to family functions with dozens of extended family members. Ozzy was close to them all. In fact, for the last six years, he had lived with his cousin, Mac, in Seattle.

Mac happened to be a successful NFL football player. He was a veteran quarterback, who played in Seattle for the Seahawks and had a mansion on Mercer Island.

Ozzy decided he wanted to study photography with a specific professor at the University of Washington, so he moved in with Mac while he went to college. Ozzy was one of the first in the family to decide to move to Seattle with Mac, but then other people moved in, and he found himself living with multiple roommates.

Three people, including Ozzy, were already living with Mac when he married a woman named Morgan. She had a daughter from a previous marriage, and they both moved into the house on Bank Street.

Even then, Ozzy stayed. There was a tiny kitchen on his side of the house that no one but he ever used. He wasn't in anyone's way there, and Mac and Morgan told him plenty of times that they wanted him to continue to live at the house as long as he lived in Seattle.

All of them thought of Galveston as home, and Ozzy hadn't planned on staying in Seattle after college, but he got discovered as a photographer, and that changed everything for him. He now worked for the rich and famous, which meant he was pretty much both of those things himself.

Ozzy dropped out of college during his last semester. If he had continued to show up to class, he would have had to turn down high-profile jobs, and he wasn't going to do that. The diploma was initially a way to help him get a job, and he figured he could go back to school later if it came to that. So, for Ozzy, a bird in the hand was worth two in the bush, and he quit school not long before he would have graduated. No one gave him a hard time about it.

Ozzy started traveling almost every week. Out of convenience, he kept his home base in Seattle rather than moving back to Galveston permanently. In the last two years he had taken nearly fifty trips all over the world to shoot on location.

Heath Vick was the Hollywood connection that put him in touch with Leonardo DiCaprio, and the shoot Ozzy did with

Leo in Paris for GQ Magazine was the spread that put his career over the top.

Ozzy had an eye for framing beautiful photographs, and his personality and style brought out candid beauty in his subjects. He knew the geometry of the face and how to find someone's most beautiful side. He could say the right things to coax their most compelling smile.

Sometimes he traveled light and worked alone. He would go on trips with famous people and take pictures of them for their own personal use. And other times, he did editorial spreads for magazines and worked with teams of professionals and assistants. Ozzy got thrown into a world of elite professional photography, and he faked it till he made it.

It had been almost two years since that shoot with Leo, and now Ozzy had finally hit his stride. He could relax and feel like he knew what he was doing when he went on trips.

He stayed focused on the mission.

His photographs featured the best in people, and that was what kept people hiring him.

Ozzy could afford to move out of Mac's and buy his own place in Seattle or in Galveston, but he had friends in Seattle, and he enjoyed living on Bank Street with all that family around. So, for now, he was staying put.

Actually, right now, at this very moment, Ozzy was back home in Galveston. He would spend a week at home with his parents, but he was leaving on the 22nd and would spend Christmas with the Kardashians, literally.

Ozzy was thinking about that upcoming trip as he tried on a hat at the local artisan's fair. He looked at his reflection in the mirror and saw his dark, unruly curly hair peeking out from underneath the hat.

"It's a stingy brim," the man said. He was the booth-keeper, and he stared at Ozzy with an appraising eye. "A stingy brim fedora," he added. "I've been making hats for twenty years, and I've only said this a handful of times, but I believe I made that hat for you, sir. I might give it to you if you don't decide to buy it."

Ozzy smiled as he went to take it off with one hand. "I think you're right, it was made for me," Ozzy said. "It feels great. I'd love to buy it from you."

The man stuck out his hand and Ozzy shifted the hat so he could shake it.

"Josiah Green," he said. "And I thank you. I think it's a wonderful choice."

The gentleman moved toward the area with the cash box where they would make the transaction for the hat.

"Ozzy Abramson," Ozzy said.

"Oh, are you one of Jenny's boys?"

"I am," Ozzy said. He almost said 'yes sir', but he couldn't quite get it out. He had been away from Texas for the last six years and he had grown accustomed to dropping the sirs and ma'ams since people in Washington seemed to take offense to it.

"My wife and I went to school with Jenny and Josh. We're a few years older than them."

5

"Oh, okay," Ozzy said, but he smiled over the man's shoulder because his mom and aunt were approaching. "There she is now, actually."

"Hey Josiah," Jenny said.

"Hi, Jenny. Lucy. How are you two ladies?"

"We're good, other than I'm here to shop for other people and I keep buying stuff for myself," Jenny said.

"You just got one thing for yourself," Lucy said.

"Are you talking about the shirt?" Jenny asked her.

"Yeah."

"What about the soap?" Jenny said.

Lucy scoffed. "Soap doesn't count," she said. "That's practical. If you're not buying it here, you'd be buying it at Walmart."

They came to stand in the booth next to Ozzy.

"What about a hat?" Ozzy said. "Is that practical?"

"Is it for you?" Jenny asked trying to peek at the bag Josiah was holding. "I thought you might be getting it for Jasmine."

"I assumed you wanted me to wrap it up and bag it," Josiah said. "I didn't even ask you if you wanted to wear it out. It looks real nice on him."

"Oh, it's for you? Cool!" Jenny said.

Ozzy was glad he didn't have to respond to the Jasmine question.

"At least try it on for us," Lucy said.

Ozzy obliged, put on the hat, and both of them loved it and told him he should wear it right then.

They spoke with Josiah for another five or ten minutes and Lucy ended up buying two hats as Christmas gifts for other people.

"Who's this Jasmine?" was the first thing Lucy said when they walked away from the booth. "Mac's mentioned that name to me a few times."

"That's because Mac knows her. She's my friend and we hang out all the time. Sometimes, on bigger jobs, I'll take her to work with me as an assistant. (He paused.) And I'm sure I will get her a Christmas present," he added nonchalantly. "But she's not my girlfriend, if that's what either of you are assuming. We're just friends."

"That's what he always says," Jenny said.

"Because it's always true," Ozzy said, smiling.

"Yeah, but there have been others like her who drop everything and follow you around, and then you—"

"I'm not leading anybody on, if that's what you're getting at."

Just then, a couple of old friends walked up to them. Ozzy and his mom and aunt talked to them for a few minutes before making their way to the booth with all the tie-dye. There were racks and racks of colorful fabric. Jenny and Lucy both wanted to buy a few tie-dye or batik items as gifts, so they stopped to do a little shopping.

"Everybody likes that new hat," Lucy said to Ozzy as they sifted through the rack, looking at shirts. "You got two compliments since you bought it." Smiling, she reached up and touched the brim of the hat with her fingertip. "You can't help it if they follow you around like puppy dogs, can you?" she said, referring to Jasmine again, unfortunately.

Ozzy just smiled and shrugged it off.

"Mac tells me about the different ones," Lucy said. "There was Anne, and then Charlotte stayed for a few years. I thought she was going to be the one. And now Jasmine."

"Yeah, again, though, Aunt Lucy, none of them were ever even my girlfriends."

"I've had this same conversation with him," Jenny said. "Because I've met them all. And they're all wonderful, and I want to take them in, and love on them, but I never know if—"

"No, Mom," Ozzy said. He shook his head thoughtfully. "I love women. I do. I love having a best friend as a woman. They're wonderful. They're artistic, and nurturing, and really industrious. I love having a woman around. Some of my best friends have been women, obviously. I just don't want any of them in my life in a way where they're… " he hesitated and peered at his aunt with a cautious expression.

"Where they're what?"

"Where they're bossing me around."

"Well, Ozzy, it doesn't feel like that when you… if that's what you're scared of, then you just haven't found the one," Lucy said. "Because it doesn't feel like bossing around when you're with the right person. Does Jasmine boss you around?"

"No. But that would change if she was my girlfriend."

"I don't know," Lucy said, sounding unconvinced.

"Lucy Klein, my darling! Oh hello, sweet Jenny, I didn't even see you. Who is this? No. Ozzy Abramson? You're kidding!"

Jenny nodded at the woman, and she reached out and hugged Ozzy, squeezing him tightly.

"Goodness, Ozzy, you are so handsome. All of your boys are gorgeous, Jenny."

"Ozzy, you remember Ms. Evelyn," Lucy said. "She's my mom's best friend."

"Sure, yes," Ozzy said, nodding. "How are you?"

"Fine, honey, I haven't seen you in so long, but heard you were doing well with your photography. Congratulations." She smiled sweetly at Ozzy.

"Thank you," he said.

"Are you staying through Christmas?"

"I have to head out a few days before. I'm here for a week, though."

"Okay, well, good. Are you still living in Seattle with Mac?"

"I am," he said, nodding.

"Oh, my goodness, wouldn't that be something? I don't know if you're busy later today, or if it could work out for you, but we were supposed to meet up at Tara's ballet studio later this afternoon. My oldest son and his family live in North Carolina, so we hardly get to see them. I have eight grandkids, but only two granddaughters, and both of them do ballet. Valerie, Thomas's youngest is in that little Angelina Ballerina class Tara puts on for the little ones. Anyway, my other granddaughter lives in Carolina, so I've had to miss most of her ballet performances." Evelyn gave them a self-deprecating smile like she was trying to get to the point. "Anyway, Evie, my namesake, my other granddaughter from North Carolina, is in town visiting for Christmas, and I wanted to get her and Valerie together for a photograph in their ballerina outfits. We planned on doing it at four o'clock this afternoon. Thomas is just going to take a picture with his camera, but wouldn't that be something if you could take it!" She smiled hopefully at Ozzy. "I'd be happy to pay you whatever you normally charge."

"Do you think you could do it?" Lucy asked.

Ozzy wasn't expecting his aunt to step in and give him those beseeching eyes.

He stuttered, thinking of a kindergarten ballet photo shoot. "Uh, I, uh, I was…"

"I told Josh and Pamela we would come over for dinner tonight," Jenny said, offering her son an excuse.

"It's okay," Evelyn said. "I just thought that it would be so neat if it worked out where you happened to be open and wanted to take a job—I'd pay you, of course."

Ozzy knew the woman was a friend of the family, so he was not going to tell her what he normally made for a photo shoot.

"He could probably think about it," Lucy said, still looking at Ozzy like she really hoped he would make it happen.

"Well, it's no big deal if you can't. And we could be flexible on the time, too. We talked about four o'clock, but we could be there at five or six, or even sometime tomorrow, if it works better for you."

"Oh, yeah, I'm sure we can work something out," Lucy said.

They took a second to say goodbye to Evelyn, and Ozzy stared at his aunt when the lady walked away.

"I'm so sorry," Lucy said, as soon as Evelyn was out of earshot. "But I love that woman with all my heart, Ozzy. She is crazy about those grandbabies of hers, and it would make her so happy to have some of your beautiful photos. Ozzy, I know she had no idea, but I'll actually seriously pay you what you normally make. I know it's a lot, and I know it's a lot to ask, but I'm willing to do it for Ms. Evelyn. She and Mister Carl have done so much for me. You should've seen the huge picnic spread she laid out when Drew and I first met. She helped him surprise me with it. I felt like a princess that day. Looking back, there was no telling how much money she spent doing that. And that was way back before I had ever released a book. She just goes out of her way for our family—has for years. I used to call on her all the time for help with Mac, and she never hesitated."

Jenny looked at Ozzy with an apologetic glance, and he shrugged and gave her a little smile. "It's fine," he said. "Just tell Ms. Evelyn I'll meet them over there today at four. I'll take a few pictures, edit them, and then email them to her. It's no big deal."

CHAPTER 2

❯❯❯❯❯❮❮❮❮❮

Evelyn "Evie" Taylor, firstborn daughter of Chris and Ronnie Taylor, granddaughter of Carl and Evelyn Taylor (Abby King's best friend).

Evie

I used to love to dance. I took ballet and jazz year-round as a child. I minored in dance during my first three years of college. But I tore my ACL and had to have surgery, so I stopped dancing and concentrated on my teaching degree. I hadn't set foot in a dance studio in almost two years when my grandma from Texas called and asked me to pose in a ballerina picture with my little cousin.

I was the firstborn grandchild, and then Evelyn and Carl had six grandsons over the course of seventeen years before having another granddaughter. Valerie, who was five now, lived in Galveston with Evelyn (whom we called Gemma), Carl, and most of my aunts, uncles, and cousins.

13

I had a few family members on my mom's side in North Carolina, but they were different—more standoffish, harder to get to know. They got together and ate meals on some of the holidays, but my relationships with them were more surface-level than the ones I had with my dad's family in Texas. I grew up anxiously looking forward to the once-a-year trips we made to see Gemma and Carl.

Note: Carl had no pet name. We simply referred to him as Carl. It was a family joke, and we said it with the utmost respect, but Carl was Carl, even to us grandkids.

There were eight grandkids on my dad's side. I had two younger brothers, Jeremy and Nate. My Uncle Noah, had two boys, Justin and Joe, and my Uncle Tom had Logan and Michael before his youngest, little Valerie, came along.

I had cousins in Galveston that spanned the ages of twelve to five. That was extra enjoyable for me because my little brothers were growing up and getting their own lives.

All this to say, I loved spending time with my family in this quaint little island town, and I figured it wouldn't kill me to try to squeeze into a costume I wore in high school if it pleased my grandmother.

The costume she requested was from a performance I had done as the Sugar Plum Fairy. Gemma asked me to wear it because she came to North Carolina to see that show and it had really made an impression on her.

She loved to watch me dance. She lived twelve hundred miles away and didn't make it to most of my performances over the years, but she always watched videos and wanted to talk to me about dance when I saw her.

So, I packed my costume and agreed to pose for a photograph with my little cousin, who apparently would be wearing something similar. I didn't give it much thought until I found myself stepping into tights.

The day had passed in a blur, and I felt a little off—displaced—out of it.

I had just come to Texas the evening before and I woke up in a different state, so that was part of it. But I had also slept until noon today, which I never did. I was in my first year as a kindergarten teacher, and I left North Carolina the day after school let out for Christmas break. I had given all of my energy to the semester, and now that I was comfortable at Gemma's, I could finally relax. I slept far too long.

I got in at eight o'clock the night before and I went to bed at eleven. I didn't wake up until noon today. I thought we were meeting Uncle Thomas and Valerie up here to take a few pictures in our costumes, which was fine, but then Gemma came home from the holiday market and informed me that we would be doing the whole thing with a real photographer.

The four hours since I woke up in a different state were somewhat dreamlike already, and now I found myself standing in the restroom of a stranger's ballet studio, stepping into an elaborate costume. I wasn't hungry when I woke up, which was good because this thing fit like a glove—a tight glove.

I brought my pointe shoes and my slippers. I decided to wear the slippers and only get out the pointe shoes if Gemma asked me to. I wore a little makeup, but nothing like the glittery stage makeup I wore in the actual production. I did pull my hair into a tight bun, though.

"Oh, you look divine," Gemma said when I opened the door.

"The photographer just got here. Everybody's in that back studio."

I straightened at the mention of the photographer and tried out a quick smile. I never took photos with a photographer. Aside from school photos, I had never encountered a photographer. My dad enjoyed taking pictures and he always set up the camera for family photos. There had never been a reason for me to hire a photographer. I was a bit nervous.

"Great," I said smiling and acting like I was comfortable.

"Thank you for going along with all this," she said as we walked down the hallway. "Valerie really looks up to you, and I think she'd cherish a photograph of you two."

Valerie was only three the last time I danced, but I was easygoing about it.

"I talked to your mom a minute ago," Gemma said. "She had tried to call you. I told her you slept in and now I'm running you around. She just wanted to check on you."

My mom, dad, and brothers would all fly to Galveston for Christmas. But I wanted to stay longer, and I wanted to have my own car while I was there, so I came early and drove myself.

"There he is... this is Ozzy Abramson. His family is dear friends of ours."

There were about five people in the room, but I knew all of the others, so there was only one guy she could be talking about. He was having a conversation with my aunt who was gesturing to Valerie. He was tall and thin. He had dark hair that hung in curls that twisted this way and that. It looked messy, but in the best way possible. He was handsome and young, and he looked like an actual movie star. I had envisioned that the photographer would be older and... well, female, honestly.

"That's who's taking our picture? That guy over there?"

"Ozzy, yes. He's Jenny's oldest boy. He lives up in Seattle with Mac, the football player. We've told you about their family."

They had indeed told me about this family, and I couldn't help but feel even more nervous—like I needed to make some sort of impression on him, for Gemma's sake. He turned and looked at me for a brief second before searching the area around me. He made eye contact with Gemma and his expression turned to a look of confusion.

"Who's this?" he asked with a patient smile aimed at her.

"My granddaughter," she said. "Evie, this is Ozzy, Ozzy, this is my granddaughter, Evie. Evelyn, like me." She reached out and patted my shoulder. "Isn't she beautiful?"

"S-she is beautiful," Ozzy agreed. "And about three feet taller than I expected."

"I know I was wondering how we would pose," I said, letting out a little nervous laugh.

"No, I meant just in general," he said. "I thought the cousin I was waiting on was five or six years old, like Miss Valerie."

"Oh, my goodness, did you really?" Gemma asked, with a wide-eyed expression aimed at him.

"I, I actually did," he said, looking me over seriously like he was a little stunned. I felt embarrassed, and I felt blood rush to my face. My cheeks got hot and I stooped down to adjust my slipper even though it didn't need it.

"This is even better," Ozzy said in a decisive tone. "These'll make some interesting photos. Smile at me." He paused and I glanced at him to see who he was talking to. He was looking at me and I smiled. It was a cautious smile because I wasn't sure if I was doing the right thing, but he studied me for a second, furrowing his eyebrows. "Yeah, okay, huh. Yeah, this'll be fun. I'll need to take a second to, uh, think about the window, and the lighting, but yeah, I just need a few minutes to talk to the ladies if possible—or whoever wants to be photographed. The others can wait in the hall."

My aunt and uncle were in the room, along with both of my cousins and one of their friends. Gemma was also there, so it was too packed. Ozzy was no-nonsense and sure of himself, and I was thankful for that in a moment where I felt like my confidence and/or desire to do this was wavering.

"I'll take the boys to the diner on the corner to get a milkshake," my grandma said.

"I'll go with you," Thomas agreed.

Aunt Joan gave Valerie a reluctant stare like she wasn't quite sure about leaving.

"You can stay if you need to," Ozzy said.

"She'll be fine," I said, not wanting Joan to stand there and watch us the whole time.

"I will," Valerie agreed, wanting to be a good girl. "But I want a milkshake."

"We'll bring you one when you're done," Uncle Thomas assured her. "Strawberry?"

Valerie nodded excitedly and they all began milling about getting ready to leave the room.

Gemma spoke to Ozzy and Aunt Joan spoke to Valerie.

The boys played tag in the middle of the room, their sneakers screeching on the wood floors. Uncle Thomas scolded them.

There were a few seconds of chaos where I just stood there in the middle of the room, wearing a tutu.

Before I knew it, though, they were all leaving the room, and it was just Valerie, Ozzy, and me. He introduced himself to us again. He had an easy way about him. He was so calm, relaxed, and confident that it was impossible to be upset or flustered around him. He put us both at ease. He moved us around, telling us to do certain things and look certain ways. He instructed us nonstop, and he did it in a way that made it sound like he was constantly pleased with what he saw. The photoshoot I had been so nervous about turned out to be a piece of cake.

Ozzy talked us through everything. He was forthright with his instructions, and we simply did what he said as he snapped photos. It was easy. The room was quiet except for Ozzy's voice and the low, muffled music coming from the class next door.

Ozzy spoke to us the whole time, not just instructing us, but also telling us tidbits of information about himself. We smiled and laughed at his stories, and we were serious when he would say something interesting. I couldn't help but think he shared certain things with us in order to evoke certain reactions. We moved and posed in different ways for about twenty minutes.

Ozzy moved around us the whole time. He did things like lie on the floor and take pictures of our reflections in the mirror from across the room.

I was reluctant when I first met Ozzy, but he completely put me at ease. I had no idea how any of these pictures would come out, but I didn't really care because I had fun taking them. Valerie and I were both so comfortable with him. We did what he told us to do, and just like that, he stood up and said we were done.

I had been in a sitting pose, and Ozzy made eye contact with me and held out his hand to help me up.

"Oh, okay, really? That's it?" I said.

"Yeah, I got about four hundred photos just now."

I put my hand in his, and he pulled me up. We were finished, and suddenly I felt weird for wearing a costume. I sprang to my feet and gave him a little bow and smile.

"Thank you," I said. "We'll go change. I'll go change. Val might not want to... Val, do you want to change? Valerie?"

She was preoccupied with watching herself in the mirrors and didn't even seem like she heard me.

"I'll take that as a 'no'," I said to Ozzy with a shrug. "Do you need to leave right now, or do you think you could wait in here with Val for two minutes while I go change?"

"I'll wait," he said. "I was planning on talking to Ms. Evelyn."

CHAPTER 3

> >>>>>><<<<<<

Ozzy

*O*zzy watched Evie leave the room. It was a jog, technically, but she was light on her feet and she scurried out of there in her little pink tutu like she was gliding on ice, floating on air.

What. The. Actual. Heck.

Who was this girl?

Ozzy stared at the door when it closed behind her. In his mind's eye, he went back to a few of the pictures he had taken. Ozzy was passionate about creating beautiful photographs. He spent his life thinking of ways to build a scene around a person to make them look their best. That was why he was so shaken about Evie. He was so captivated by her face that he didn't even want to build a scene. He would have sat in that room and taken four hundred pictures of her face with nothing else. He could've easily taken four hundred pictures of her mouth alone. Her eyes, too. They were expressive and they were a color green he had never seen before.

Her appearance threw him off. He was stunned by the fact that she wasn't a little kid, and then she turned out to be the most interesting looking woman he had ever seen. He had to fight the urge to make the photographs completely revolve around her. He remembered how excited the little girl's mother was and he made sure to get some photos of her, but good grief, it would have been easy to forget the little girl was there. Evelyn Taylor's oldest granddaughter was perhaps the most interesting and beautiful subject Ozzy had ever photographed. He was actually shaken from it.

He wanted to run in there and ask if he could get some more. He couldn't believe he had been reluctant about going there. Evie was extremely fun to photograph, and Ozzy was actually thankful for this photo shoot. It brought him back to the joys of why he did this in the first place. Ozzy laughed at himself for going into it thinking they should be thankful to him. He was thinking about that and packing up his camera when he heard the door open.

"I was waiting in the hall," the girl's mother said as she came inside. "I saw Evie come out, so I thought y'all might be done."

"We are," Ozzy said.

"Thank you. Did you, would you, could you get some pictures of Valerie by herself? You know, in case they came out better than the little ones Tara took of her with the class pictures."

Ozzy didn't usually find himself in situations like this. Maybe he would have normally been offended by her comparison, but he didn't have anything better to do at that moment than to take

24

a few more photos. He took out his camera and got a few more shots of the little girl while she walked around absentmindedly. He stopped when he heard someone coming.

"Oh, you're here, Aunt Joan. Good. Okay," Evie said as she came in. She was wearing jeans and a pink sweater with flats. She was not Ozzy's type at all. He had to tell himself that. She was not his type. There was no reason for him to be fascinated with her. He blamed the shock of thinking he was working with a little kid.

Evie said, more than once, that she was out of shape in regards to ballet, but Ozzy remembered the lines of her body when she held a pose, and she was not out of shape. She was in fine shape. Good shape. Great shape. That smile, though—it lit up her whole face.

Ozzy wanted to photograph her again. He ripped his gaze from hers and went to his camera bag to put up his camera before he became the weirdo who just took pictures of her for no reason. He reminded himself that he did not go out with women who dressed in pink sweaters. He noticed a tiny, gold cross pendant hanging from a delicate chain, and now Ozzy was pretty sure she wasn't his type at all.

Ozzy would call himself a Christian if you asked him. He had an experience at church when he was a teenager, and it was enough that he knew he believed in Jesus. But this girl was a ballerina-dancing, church-going, cross-wearing, pretty-dang-sheltered good girl, and Ozzy knew it. Some depraved side of him must have taken it as a challenge, because Ozzy desperately wanted to kiss her. He was pretty sure that wouldn't happen for months with a girl like that, and he told himself that was the only reason why he wanted to do it.

His mind began to spin. Ozzy was not used to these types of feelings. He had kissed women in his life, but he was not usually the initiator.

"Thomas is outside with Val's ice cream," Joan said to Evie. "But we didn't know what you wanted, so Gemma's waiting at the diner for you."

Ozzy glanced her way and realized she wasn't talking to him.

Joan saw Ozzy look that way and said, "I'm sure Gemma would want to get you a milkshake, too. If you want one. She told me to tell you that she would text you and go by your mom's house sometime later this evening to settle up with you for the photos. Do you think, if I give you my email address, you could maybe email some of these pictures later tonight?"

"I won't have anything ready for you to look at tonight, but yes, I'll email them to Ms. Evelyn as soon as I can, and she can forward them to you."

"Okay, well I'm going to take Gemma up on that milkshake," Evie said with a smile. She waved at Ozzy. "Thank you so much for making that easy. It was nice meeting you."

His chest felt tight.

"I'll head over there with you," he said. "Are you going to Carson's Diner?"

"Yes," she said, looking a little surprised. She held up the plastic garment bag. "I just have to stop at my car for a second, but it's on the way."

"Okay, I'll walk over there with you so I can talk to Ms. Evelyn."

"Well, we're coming with you if we're done here," Joan said.

But she and her family met up outside of the ballet studio, which was a block away from the diner. They already had Valerie's ice cream, so they decided not to go back that way.

Ozzy and Evie were now alone, and they walked across the street headed toward the diner.

"I heard you say you were from North Carolina," Ozzy said, walking beside her.

"I am. Fayetteville area."

"And you're a teacher?"

"Yes. Kindergarten. I'm in my first year—one semester in."

"When do you have time for ballet?" he asked.

She laughed. "Never."

"What's that mean?" he asked.

"It means I never dance anymore. I haven't put on these slippers in two years. I couldn't even find my tights. I had to buy new ones."

"Oh, I just, well, with the way your grandma talked, I thought you were still really into it."

"No. I just did that for her. She used to love to watch me dance, so she wanted a picture of us together."

"Why don't you do it anymore?" he asked.

"Torn ACL."

"Oooh. Sorry. Surgery?"

"Yeah. My junior year of college."

"Why didn't you get back into it?"

"Because college was over by the time I rehabbed enough to feel good."

"Why can't you dance somewhere else?"

"I don't know. I never really thought about that. I assumed I was done when I finished college. I was just minoring in it, anyway."

Evie went to a practical little silver car that might as well have come with the teaching job. Ozzy tried to have sarcastic thoughts about her, but it wasn't working at all. The pink sweater, the little compact silver car, all of it was somehow appealing when it went with her.

"Are you getting ice cream, or are you just coming to talk to Gemma?" Evie asked as she closed the door.

"Why? What are you doing?"

"Oh, I, I was asking because I didn't know if you wanted to stop at your car." She motioned to the camera bag Ozzy was carrying like she thought he would want to put it away.

"No, I'll take it with me, just so nothing happens to it," he said.

There was no way he was letting it out of his sight. He got some amazing captures during this photo shoot. There was this sequence of photographs of Evie that he thought might include one of the best pictures he had ever taken. It was beautiful, pristine, definitely magazine quality—fine art. There was no way he was leaving the camera in the car.

"This place," she said as they walked.

Ozzy looked where she was pointing, and saw Bank Street Boxing. Mac's house on Bank Street in Seattle was only purchased because Mac had an affinity for streets named Bank. That all started with the *Bank Street* in Galveston, down which they were currently walking. Ozzy's family owned houses and businesses all up and down Bank Street, especially on this block. The ballet studio and the boxing gym were both owned by the Castros, Billy and his daughter, Tara.

"That gym is my uncle... I know everybody at that gym. The guy who owns it... Billy Castro... he's not technically my uncle, but we're connected by marriage, and me and my brothers, we're so close to him that we call him Uncle Billy."

"Oh, do you do boxing?" Evie asked, pulling back and looking at Ozzy with newfound interest. "Because I *really* wanted to try it. I told my grandma if I ever move over here, that's the first place I'd go. It seems like so much fun, doesn't it?" She peered inside as they walked past the windows and then she turned to smile at Ozzy. "I don't want to get into a fight with anybody or anything. I just think it'd be fun to punch and kick one of those bags. Gemma said they have all kinds of classes there. My brother's friend has one of those bags, and I tried it one time, but it really hurt my hand. I think you have to wear gloves."

Ozzy let out a little laugh. "You definitely have to wear gloves," he said. "Those bags are hard."

"Do you know about boxing? Ahh, that would be so cool if I could box. Like in Million Dollar Baby when she was carrying the tray, working on her footwork. I always thought boxing was so cool." She looked at him with a playful smirk. "Not the fighting part, just the... training. You know, like Million Dollar

Baby. Not the end of that movie, though. I didn't watch the end because I knew what happened, but that first part... when she's training... so good." Evie had a look in her eyes like she wanted so badly to try boxing.

"I'll take you in the gym right now if you want to go," Ozzy said, stepping in front of her as they walked. They had been approaching the gym's front door, and he reached out like he was about to grab the handle, but she stepped back, shaking her head and smiling at Ozzy.

"No, no, not right now. I'm not going in there now. I just said I'd do it if I ever moved here. The chances of that happening are like... one in... four... so I don't want to rush things."

"One in *four*?" Ozzy said, letting out a little laugh.

"Yeah, one in four."

"That you'll move here? Those are actually really good odds. Are you thinking about moving? How do you get one in four odds that you're going to move somewhere? I thought you were about to say that the chances of it happening were like one in a million or something. One in four? That actually might happen."

She shrugged. "Yeah, well, it's up to me," she said. "I've been thinking about it for a while now. I've never moved out of my parents' house. I'd be moving in with Gemma and Carl and getting a job as a teacher, I'm sure. So, I'm not sure if it'd be worth uprooting just to get into the same exact situation I'm in now. That's why I'm seventy-five percent sure I'll stay in North Carolina."

"What about the other twenty-five? What draws you here? Is it just the boxing gym?"

"No, that's only like one or two percent," she said. "Three, if I just watched Rocky."

"What is it then?"

"I don't know. Adventure I guess. And family. Family is a lot of it. I have one brother who went off to college last year and another one who will go off next year. Jeremy left in August. He's going to school at Clemson. And Nate's going into the military. I'm going through empty nest syndrome, and I'm barely twenty-three. There's a small part of me that thinks I need to get out of my parents' house. Even if it's into a similar situation. Thank you," she added when he opened the door for her.

She had been speaking slowly, so they made it down the sidewalk and to the diner. Ozzy opened the door for her, and she walked inside, waving when she spotted Evelyn who was standing at the counter with the waitress and cook.

"Oh, Ozzy, you came, too! I'll buy you both some ice cream. Or dinner. That'd be great. It's almost dinnertime. Why don't y'all do that? Maggie's got my card information. She'll just charge it to me."

"You don't have to do that," Ozzy said.

"Oh, I want to, sweetheart," Evelyn said, giving him a sideways hug. "I can't thank you enough for taking photos of my granddaughters."

"It really was... fine. It worked out with... everything." Ozzy didn't know what he was saying. He normally didn't find himself tongue-tied, and he took a second to gather his thoughts and consider whether he should sit down for dinner at 4:30pm. He cleared his throat. "We had brunch this morning at that market, and I haven't eaten since. I'm not trying to put it on your tab or anything, Ms. Evelyn, but I actually might sit here and eat. You're welcome to join me, if you want, either of you."

Evelyn sighed and smiled as she patted Evie on the shoulder. "I'm going to leave that to my granddaughter, and yes, it most certainly is my treat. And this is for you, Ozzy," she added. "I was going to run it to your mom's house, but I can just hand it to you. Thank you very much." Evelyn had a check written and folded neatly in her pocket, and she took it out and thrust it toward Ozzy before he knew what was happening. He took it and thanked her because he didn't know what else to do. He wanted to argue, but he figured he could just tell her later that he wouldn't cash it.

Ozzy didn't contemplate how weird it was that he was thinking of not cashing the check or what that meant in regard to his feelings for Evie. He had so enjoyed taking pictures of her that he now had an aversion to taking money for it.

He knew that was unlike him, so he took the folded piece of paper and tucked it into his pocket with a thankful smile and nod.

"Thank you," he said. "But I'll get dinner. At least for myself, and if Evie stays."

"Oh, no, dinner's on me," Evelyn said. "Maggie and I go way back. She'll set you up and send me the bill. It's my pleasure."

Evelyn glanced at Evie. "Do you think you'll stay with Ozzy?" she asked.

Ozzy knew she was just talking about eating, but that phrase made his heart start to race.

"Yes, I do," Evie said, making it race even more.

CHAPTER 4

Evie

I was still tired from the trip, and the semester, and the odd thirteen hours of sleep I got the night before. Plus, I was out of it from having a non-existent morning. They asked if I wanted to stay at the restaurant for an early dinner, and I agreed.

"It feels like lunchtime to me right now, honestly, so yes, I wouldn't mind having some food." I looked at Ozzy when I said that, and he smiled.

"Okay, it's settled, then," Gemma said. "Y'all sit wherever you like and Maggie will take care of you." She hugged me and walked out, and Ozzy motioned toward the nearby stools.

"Did you want to sit at the counter, or grab a booth?"

"A stool's fine," I said, since it was closer and seemed like a good option.

"Sit anywhere you like," the waitress said as she took off to tend to someone else. I had met Ms. Maggie before, with

Gemma and Carl. She was always at this diner. Ozzy must have had the same thought because he mentioned her.

"Ms. Maggie is here every time I come," he said as we chose a place to sit. "She doesn't change. I think she might live here."

I laughed a little at the thought as I sat down. Ozzy took the spot next to me. I took my purse off of my shoulder and settled it near my feet before turning and smiling at him. My eyes met his and it felt like the first time I noticed what color they were.

"Wow, your eyes are really dark," I said, causing him to smile.

"You're just noticing?" he asked.

"Yeah, I'm just noticing," I said, staring.

"Yeah, brown," Ozzy said, shifting a menu to where it was in front of me.

I glanced down at it. I was just starting to skim the breakfast section when he spoke again.

"You were saying you might move here because you have an empty nest."

I laughed. "It's not my nest, technically, but yes, it's different there with Jeremy gone. And Nate knows he's leaving in a few months, too, so he's spending a bunch of time with his friends and girlfriend. I'm not planning on staying with my parents forever, it just kind of worked out that it was more convenient for me to stay there than to move anywhere else."

"I hear you," Ozzy said. "That's kind of the same boat I'm in."

"Do you still live with your parents? I thought you said you lived in Seattle."

"I do, but I live with my cousin, Mac. The one who plays football."

"That's right," I said.

"I was planning on moving back here after college, but I travel so much that it's hard to justify taking the time to relocate. Plus, Mac won't be in Seattle forever, and we'll all be looking at moving back at some point, I'm sure."

I glanced at him. "Oh, you're moving back here?"

"Yeah," he said. "For sure. It's a cool town. There's not as much going on here as Seattle, obviously, but there's a certain charm to it."

"You think?" I said sarcastically, smiling at him.

"Why do you say it like that?" he asked.

"Because. Look around yourself—I've never been in such a cool place. Roy Orbison playing on the jukebox? Every time I come in here, it's doo-wop and milkshakes, and sticking to the plan, solid as a rock. Old school. This whole street is like this. These Victorian buildings are amazing. That building with the ballet studio, and then the boxing gym. I could just live down here on Bank Street." I spun around one time on my stool as I was saying that, just to illustrate my point, and Ozzy laughed.

"We all grew up loving Bank Street, too. That's why Mac bought that house on Mercer Island. It was too big for him and he still bought it because of the name of the street it was on."

"Is the fact that it's too big for him the reason why you get to live there?"

"Yes, it actually is, "Ozzy said.

"Well, I guess it's good he likes the name Bank Street."

"I'm so sorry, y'all," Maggie said coming back to us. "I went over there for a second and got held up. I'm glad you got some menus. Can I get an appetizer started for you, or something to drink?"

"We know what we want to order, if you're ready," Ozzy said.

"Yes, sir, I'm certainly ready," Maggie said.

I was not ready. I hadn't even looked at the menu. I had barely even read the word *breakfast*. I was hungry but I was also preoccupied.

"We'll have two coffees, two waters, and two milkshakes, one vanilla and one chocolate."

"Got it. And to eat?"

"A meatloaf with mac and cheese and mashed potatoes."

"And for the lady?" she asked.

"A fried chicken sandwich," Ozzy said.

"French fries or chips with the sandwich?" she asked.

Ozzy, who hadn't included me in any of this so far, looked at me and I instinctually said, "French fries."

Maggie thanked us and walked off, and I smiled at Ozzy. "At first, I thought you were getting all that for yourself and then I realized that you were ordering for me, too."

"I figured I'd order some options then you can just choose what you want. Those are two of the best things on the menu. I know I looked at you about the fries, but you can have the meatloaf if you want."

"All of that sounded amazing," I said smiling. "But you're right, I thought when you looked at me about the French fries, that meant I was stuck with the chicken sandwich."

"No," he said shaking his head easily. "Do you want the meatloaf? I'd be happy to eat the chicken sandwich."

"I don't really care," I said smiling at him. "I was just going to eat what you gave me."

"I'll give you any of it. All of it. We'll order something else if that wasn't what you wanted. I was just trying to order so we could discuss the fact that you're moving here."

"Whoa now, I didn't say I was moving here."

"Well, you said you *probably* were. You said all that about Bank Street and Roy Orbison, and you spun around on your stool, so I thought you were talking yourself into it."

I laughed. "Maybe once you move here I'll come so you can introduce me to everyone at the boxing gym," I said, lightheartedly.

"I'll do that today," he said. "We'll walk over there and I'll introduce you to everyone."

I didn't think I'd take him up on it, but I was thankful for the offer.

Ozzy and I ended up splitting the food. I took the chocolate milkshake and gave him the vanilla, but the food, we split. He cut the chicken sandwich right down the middle, and I wasn't shy about eating my half. He tried to give me half of the meatloaf also, but I just asked for a little piece since the sandwich was huge. It was all delicious, and we talked and stared straight ahead as we ate. Both of us were the oldest of three siblings, and we told stories of our home life. His twin brothers were only a year younger than him, so they had been really close growing up.

It was way later in our conversation when he mentioned that tonight he was supposed to meet up with David and Alec to play some music together. My brothers were not at all musically inclined and I couldn't imagine playing music with them. I wanted to ask the specifics of what they were playing, but our conversation was interrupted by someone who knew Ozzy and came up to talk to us.

We spoke with that guy for about ten minutes. He knew my dad and my uncles, and he talked to me some, too. That was the way things were on this little street—I wasn't surprised to meet someone who knew Evelyn and Carl's family and asked me enough questions to figure out that I was connected to them.

Ozzy and I went on talking about something else after that guy left, and I didn't get to ask him about playing music with his brothers. We tried to pay for our food, but Maggie insisted that Evelyn had already taken care of it.

I didn't necessarily feel like leaving, but it was almost dinnertime now, and the place was beginning to fill up. Ozzy and I figured we shouldn't take up room at the counter. We thanked Maggie, tipped her, and told her goodbye before making our way out of the diner.

Ozzy saw someone else he knew as he held the door open for me. He waved at them, but didn't go over there to talk.

"Where did you park?" I asked.

"I'm in my dad's truck," he said. "It's right over there."

"Okay, well, this has been fun, Ozzy. Thank you. It was nice meeting you."

"Oh," he said, looking surprised.

I thought he was going to say something else, but he left it at that. He just looked at me, and I smiled.

"Do you want me to walk you to your truck?" I asked.

"Why wouldn't I walk you to yours?" he asked.

"Because yours is closer."

He stood there and stared at me for a few brief seconds before saying, "I'm trying to think of when I can see you again."

His words made a wave of something warm hit me. For a second, it felt like he was looking at me like he was interested in me. But this was the same guy who was headed to Christmas with the Kardashians. Ozzy wasn't trying to show off, but that little fact had come out when we were talking just now. I didn't want to be sheltered and naïve. I had talked to Ozzy for the last hour. I knew he had women in his life, and I knew he lived a travel and social media lifestyle that had left me in the dust long ago.

I thought he was a great photographer, and I had a lot of fun talking to him at the diner, but I just assumed this would be our only encounter. It was an odd feeling when we were parting ways and Ozzy actually looked a little sad about it.

It was like when I was a kid and I had a brief fantasy that I was a princess or that Justin Timberlake loved me. I imagined Ozzy pursuing me, and it gave me that same gut-tingling feeling.

"I'm here through Christmas," I said. "There's no telling when we'll run into each other."

"Oh, so, we're just leaving it to chance? You're good with that? Because I thought you might want to come see me play bass tonight."

"Are you playing bass tonight?"

He nodded.

"Bass guitar?"

He smiled and nodded again.

"Seriously? Where? You mentioned that you were doing something with your brothers tonight but I didn't get to ask about it. What's going on? Do you guys have a band?"

"They have a band. I'm not in it. But their bass player can't be at the rehearsal tonight so they asked me to sit in with them."

"Are you playing a concert?"

"No, gosh, I hope not. I'm not ready for all that. My brothers are actually really good. They've been at it a long time. The band is new, but all those guys are really good. I'm just filling in with them so they can practice. It's at Aiden's house."

"Oh, well, w-were you asking me to go to the practice?" I asked, trying not to be awkward.

We walked slowly toward his truck. "Yes, I am," he said. "It's not a big deal. I just thought if you wanted to have real-life adventures, you could go over there with me tonight."

I smiled at him. "Oh, real life adventures? Now you're trying to tempt me with adventure?"

"Is it working?" he asked.

"What kind of music is it?" I asked.

42

He grinned at me as he opened the truck door. "Does it matter?" he asked, stashing his bag on the seat.

"Kind of."

"What kind of music would make you *not* come?" he asked.

I thought about that for a second, and then tentatively, in a high-pitched voice said, "Death... metal?" I was so uncertain when I said it that Ozzy laughed.

"It's not death metal."

"Is it regular metal?" I asked, knowing that wasn't my favorite type of music.

"No," he said. "Nor is it heavy metal. It's not metal at all. There's nothing metal about it. I guess I'd call it rock if I had to say, but it's not heavy or anything. A bunch of ladies go to their concerts, if that makes you feel better. They seem to enjoy it."

"Is there singing?" I asked.

"Yes," Ozzy said, smiling at me. "It's mostly my brother, David. Alec sings sometimes, too. It's their project. That's why they're roping me into going tonight. They've been doing it for years—the whole time I've been in Seattle."

"I'd just be in the way at something like that," I said. "But thank you for the invitation. That does sound like quite the adventure."

"Then come," he said.

"Really?" I asked doubtfully, blinking at him from my place on the curb.

"If it sounds like an adventure, then you should think about coming with me."

CHAPTER 5

Five months later

Ozzy

"Dang, Ozzy what's gotten into you? I thought you were Mac in here. Shoot, son, dang. You're looking swole, Ozzy."

Justin Teague came into the weight room at Mac's house, looking surprised. Justin was a teammate of Mac's, an MVP running back who had been at the very top of his game in the years since he signed with the Seahawks. Justin was also a roommate of theirs on Bank Street in Seattle, and he was married to Mac's sister (Ozzy's cousin), Katie.

Justin and Katie had a house in Galveston, and they had been there for the last two months, so Justin had been out of the loop with Ozzy's fitness progress.

"Are y'all back for good?" Ozzy asked, turning down the music.

"No, just for the weekend, and then we're going back to Galveston for a few more weeks. I had to come in to sign a

45

contract renewal and do a press conference. I didn't think you were here. I thought you were going to London."

"I just got back last night," Ozzy said. "I met the other Ozzy."

"Osbourne?" Justin asked.

"Yeah. I also trained at Connor McGregor's gym when I was over there. I met him, too. But he had no idea who I was. I was just some big, sweaty mess of a white belt."

The timer went off, and Justin looked at Ozzy with a guilty expression. Ozzy shook his head as he put away his boxing gloves. "I was wrapping up. There was only a minute on the clock when you came in, and that was an extra round, anyway."

Justin came that way, staring at Ozzy with great interest as he packed up. "Son, Ozzy, what's gotten into you? Katie told me you were sticking with that martial arts stuff, but dang. What are you lookin' so swole for? You gettin' all G'd up for that woman in Carolina?"

"Why, do I look bigger? I was wondering. I thought my clothes might be shrinking."

Justin laughed at that and pushed at his shoulder as they began to walk out of the home gym and down the hall toward the center of the house.

"You must see yourself in the mirror," Justin said as they approached one. "You've got gains, Ozzy."

"Yeah, I guess. I don't know." Ozzy glanced at himself in the mirror as they passed it. He was bigger. He knew it. "I didn't really get into it for that so I haven't been noticing. But I do kind of need to go clothes shopping. I was just trying to get better at boxing at first, but then I found jiu jitsu. I love doing it, so I guess being in the gym is just causing me to build muscle."

"How's that going?" Justin asked. "I remember you had been going to that MMA gym a lot while we were still wrapping up the season."

"Yeah, it's been about five months."

"Wow, you could probably whip my rear end by now."

Ozzy just smiled. "It's going good, though. I'm training over at Northwest Top Team when I'm in Seattle. They have serious athletes over there. Professional fighters, like Uncle Billy's gym, but more MMA."

"Billy's adding some MMA," Justin said.

"He told me that," Ozzy agreed, nodding. "I'm nowhere near their skill level, but I'm learning. I'm trying to get as good as possible before I go to Galveston. I'm supposed to give Evie boxing lessons."

"All to impress this woman?" Justin asked.

Ozzy shrugged. "It started that way, maybe. I told her if she ever decided to move to Galveston I would meet her over at Uncle Billy's gym and work with her at boxing."

"And now she's moving?"

"Yeah."

"And you don't know how to box?"

Ozzy laughed. "I didn't, no. I knew a little just from being around my family so much, but no. Evie told me she was going to move on the summer break, and I thought, *well I better learn how to box if I'm expecting to show her.*" Ozzy smiled at Justin. "Then, I just started to like it. I got hooked. Not just on boxing, but the wrestling stuff, too. That's why I go to all those gyms now when I travel. I train like five or six days a week."

"Whoa, Ozzy," Katie said when they rounded the corner. "What were you doing in there? Working out? Goodness, you have so many muscles."

Katie was in the kitchen, and she crossed the room toward Ozzy as she was talking. She hugged him and he reluctantly half-hugged her back.

"I'm sweaty," he said.

"I don't care," she protested. "I haven't seen you in weeks."

Ozzy turned and hugged Katie tightly, causing her to squeal. "Gosh, Ozzy. Those muscles. You feel like… Justin. Your shoulders." Katie made an amazed expression as she pulled back and then squeezed Ozzy's shoulders. "What's going on here?"

"I was just telling him that," Justin said.

"I knew you were getting into martial arts, but I didn't know you, like," she looked him over, "had all this going on."

"He even goes to gyms when he travels. He met Connor McGregor."

"Barely," Ozzy said. "And he wasn't even that nice."

"He did meet Ozzy Osbourne," Justin said.

"I did meet Ozzy. And the Queen," Ozzy added.

"What? Of England? You're lying," Katie said.

He shook his head. "I met her. I shook her hand. I was photographing some horses for a friend of Ozzy's, and she came to look at using one of his studs. I was introduced along with five other people. Totally forgettable, I'm sure. But yeah, I met the Queen briefly. Very briefly."

"What does your lady friend in Carolina think of you meeting the Queen?" Katie asked. "Have you talked to her since then? Does she know?"

He smiled. "I talked to her last night, and, yes, I told her I met the Queen."

"Would you say you talk to her every day?" Katie asked.

"The Queen? I barely met her."

Katie scowled playfully at Ozzy for misunderstanding intentionally.

"No, we don't talk every day," Ozzy said "I don't know how much we talk. I hadn't thought about it. I like her, but I don't keep track of how much we talk."

"You're being too easygoing about this," Katie said. "You either like her or you don't. I saw Jasmine leaving here a few minutes ago. That's how we knew you were in the weight room."

"She likes to work out while I'm in there," Ozzy said. "But we don't interact. She uses the rower and the elliptical."

"How does your friend in Carolina feel about that?"

"Evie? Fine."

"Fine?" Katie asked, looking surprised.

"What do you mean? Why would she care? It's not like we have any sort of commitment. We're just talking—not even."

"You and Evie, or you and Jasmine?"

"What? Neither. I'm just friends with both of them. You can have a girl who's a friend."

She smiled. "Can you?"

"Yes. Nobody's misleading anyone. I'm still just single-old-Ozzy."

"Yeah but now you can beat up anyone who questions it," Justin said.

They stood around with Katie. Ozzy needed a shower, and would go do that soon, but it had been a while and it was good to see them. "I don't know about all that," he said to Justin. "But I've talked to Uncle Billy more in the last three months than I have in years."

"Why have you been talking to him?" Katie asked. "Are you calling to ask him questions about boxing?"

Ozzy nodded. "He checks on me. I told him I was picking it up, and he calls to make sure I'm sticking with it. I end up asking him questions, though. He knows about jiu jitsu even though he's mostly a boxer. They're adding it at their gym, like Justin was saying."

"Yeah, he's bringing in a new guy to teach it," Justin said. "But I didn't know Ozzy was going all Mike Tyson on us. And all this is over a girl."

Ozzy thought about why he started, and he let it come out of his mouth as soon as it crossed his mind. "It was those pictures that did it," he said.

"What pictures?" Katie asked.

"Back at Christmas, in Galveston."

"Oh, those ballet pictures?"

"Yes," Ozzy said. "Evie. I think she's a really interesting subject to photograph. Fascinating, really. There were a few from the set that I didn't even give to Ms. Evelyn because they were just too... they were my best work, honestly. My favorite photos I've ever taken. The way I captured her face, it's like a Mona Lisa thing. I don't know how else to describe it."

"Can I see them?" Katie said.

"No," Ozzy replied in such a matter-of-fact tone that Justin laughed. "A few of them, I haven't shown anybody," he said. "One of them, I probably never will. We hung out three different times at Christmas and I never even showed them to her. I put away my camera and my computer and we just hung out. She's just a friendly girl, like Ms. Evelyn—easy to be around. I practiced with David and Alec's band at Aiden's a few times while Marc was out of town, and she liked to come with me to those."

"Does she like you?" Katie asked. "Did she move to Galveston because you asked her to? Because girls do that kind of stuff for you, Ozzy."

"Katie, don't," Justin said.

"What? They do. I'm just telling him because I don't think he always notices. One time, Charlotte quit her job because Ozzy asked her to help on a photo shoot and her boss wouldn't give her the day off."

"I did not ask her to quit," Ozzy said.

"I know, but I don't think you realize sometimes when girls are wanting you to notice them. Jasmine is definitely wanting that," Katie added.

"He's got it, Katie," Justin said.

"Yeah, I've got it, Katie," Ozzy said smirking at her.

"Do you, though?" she said. "You seem like you like this one back. You're getting all beefcaked out for her."

Ozzy laughed. "One, this beefcake-ed-ness isn't for anyone… it's a byproduct of a new hobby. And, also, I don't think I've quite reached beefcake status yet." He smiled. "I might be out of the cross-country team category, but I'm not quite a beefcake."

Katie and Justin both laughed at that.

"When is she going there? Did she already move?" Katie asked.

"No. She's moving in two weeks. She's wrapping up school."

Katie nodded. "Oh, that's right. I forgot she was a teacher. What is it? May? I've only been away from school for one year, and I'm already off schedule. Is she getting a job in Galveston?"

"Yes. She already has one."

"Where?" Katie asked.

"Crestview."

"What grade?"

"Kindergarten. She's going there to live by her grandma. Why so many questions?"

"I don't know. I've just never seen you so…" Katie scanned his appearance. "…muscle-y."

"This has nothing to do with the girl, but…" Ozzy was being silly when he curled his arms in front of him and flexed, but Katie gasped.

"Gosh, Ozzy. You're seriously lookin' really tough."

"Seriously, though," Ozzy said to her. "I'm not obsessing about Evie with the whole boxing thing. I just didn't want to embarrass myself when I told her I'd take her to Uncle Billy's gym. She's a nice girl, but I don't think of her like that. I'm doing MMA because I like it now."

CHAPTER 6

A month later

Evie

I had only lived in Galveston for two weeks, and I already loved it. Ozzy Abramson was one of my first friends. He didn't live there, but being friends with him gave me the confidence to meet other people my age. I knew my family, but my aunts and uncles were older than me and my cousins were younger than me, so my goal moving there was to meet a few friends.

That was completely effortless because Evelyn had wonderful friends who had children my age. These people were all Ozzy's friends and family. I had gone out to eat one time with Bri and Caroline, both of whom were connected to Ozzy by marriage.

Gemma had introduced me to a couple of guys as well. She was also the person who introduced me to Bri and Caroline, so I told myself she was just trying to help me make friends, which I knew was the truth. The guys were young, handsome, and single, though, and Gemma smiled a little more when she introduced me to them than she did with the girls.

Ozzy was happy when I told him I met Bri. They had lived together at Mac's for so long that he missed her now that she was back in Galveston full-time. I told him about Bri and Caroline, and the other girls Gemma introduced me to, but I never mentioned the guys.

It didn't matter, anyway. It had been a week or two since I spoke with him, and with good reason. A woman named Jasmine answered his phone one time when I called. I tried to call him but he didn't pick up, and then she instantly Facetimed me back. She was in his bedroom, lying across the foot of his bed. She introduced herself as his girlfriend and then said he was taking a shower. She asked if she could give him a message and I refused, obviously.

Things had changed with Ozzy and me since then. I didn't think I was anything more than friends with Ozzy, so I wasn't mad at him for keeping that other woman from me, but I also didn't feel right talking to him so much when he was actively seeing someone.

He traveled all the time, and I was getting settled in Galveston, so it was easy to avoid his calls. I still liked Ozzy, but I knew it was best for me to keep my distance so there wouldn't be confusion with his girlfriend. I figured he had been placed in my life to help me make the decision to move and also feel more comfortable meeting people in Galveston. I was thankful to him for that, and I still considered him a friend. That was why I smiled when Sam mentioned his name.

Samuel King: Evan and Izzy's oldest son, Ozzy's cousin, and Evelyn's not-so-subtle third attempt at marrying me off. Sam was a really nice guy, though. He said his family called him Samuel but most of his friends called him Sam, and I could choose either.

I was currently sitting across from him, smiling contentedly. We had no marriage plans, but it had been an enjoyable hour of my life. I didn't mind sharing a meal with him. I thought he was a nice guy.

We were at a booth in Carson's diner. Gemma had ended up here with the two of us and paid for this meal, much the same as she did with Ozzy and me. I had to wonder if that had been a setup, too. I was having a fine time with Sam, but I forgot he was Ozzy's cousin, so it threw me off when he mentioned him.

"What'd you say about Ozzy?" I asked.

"I said he's in."

"In what?"

"In town," Sam said. "My mom told me he got here last night. I thought you were friends with him."

"I am," I said.

I had a call from Ozzy this morning that I hadn't answered, but I had no idea he was in Galveston. My heart ached at the thought of him being in Galveston. I had a crush on Ozzy before the whole girlfriend-answering-the-phone thing, and it was easy to ignore while he was in Seattle, Europe, Canada, or Jamaica. But Galveston? He hadn't mentioned coming to Galveston in June.

"I heard from him this morning, but I missed his call," I said. "That's cool that he's in town. It'd be wonderful if he brought his girlfriend."

"What'd you say?" Sam asked since I had mumbled. He was smiling at me.

"I said it's cool that he's in town."

"Oh, I thought you said something about his girlfriend. I didn't even know Ozzy had a girlfriend. I thought he was going around the world being a single dude."

"He is," I said. "But I guess he also has a girlfriend. And he's into MMA now," I added, for no reason.

Sam smiled. He was nice and so easy to talk to that I almost told him about Jasmine and the fact that she Facetimed me. My mouth was open and I was about to say the words, but I decided not to. I didn't want Sam to know how close I was to Ozzy. Sam said his name again, but I was thinking about stopping myself from saying that, so I didn't hear him.

I made eye contact with Sam from across the booth. "What did you say?"

"I said there's Ozzy right there."

I started looking around as soon as Sam said that.

"He's outside," Sam said. "I saw him on the sidewalk a minute ago."

My heart raced as I turned and looked for him. I was excited to see him since it had been so long, but it also felt odd that things had been distant between us lately. I honestly didn't know what to expect from this interaction. I wasn't even sure there would be an interaction. Maybe he was just walking by on the sidewalk and I wouldn't encounter him at all.

I was telling myself that when I caught sight of Ozzy coming through the door of the diner. My nerves and adrenaline instantly spiked. I blinked.

He looked so different. He had gone from lanky to muscular. He has always been a cool guy, but he had a different confidence about him now. I could see it from across the restaurant. Or maybe that was just him being upset. He definitely looked focused, determined.

"Ozzy's looking different," Sam said. "I think he got a haircut."

"It's the MMA," I said, staring at him as he approached. He was about six or eight tables away when we made eye contact, and he just kept looking at me as he walked our way.

"Hey," he said.

Oh, my goodness. He was a sight to behold. It had been six months since I had seen him. *How could a man fill out like this in that time?* He wasn't stocky, but there was a layer of muscle that gave him a totally different look. He was extremely masculine, and I felt breathless at the sight of him. I swallowed and smiled and tried to think of something to say.

"Hi."

I went with 'hi'.

I smiled tentatively and Ozzy wore a cautious, serious expression as he sat down next to Sam, causing Sam to scoot over. They turned to greet each other, doing the nodding thing that guys do.

"What are you doing here with Evie?" Ozzy said, talking to Sam but shifting to look at me as he spoke. "What are you doing here with Samuel?"

"Samuel sounds so formal," I said, my face cracking into a grin.

"That's his name," Ozzy said, turning to look at Sam.

"I told her a lot of people call me Sam," Sam said.

Ozzy hesitated, looking surprised for a second before turning to stare at me. "I tried to call you. I wanted to talk to you about a photo project."

"Oh, really?"

"Yeah. I knew I was going to be in town, and I wanted to see if you could help me out with something, but it's fine. I'm only here for a few days, so if our schedule doesn't line up… it's not… the end… of the world…"

Ozzy spoke slowly, and it was extremely awkward. My heart was pounding and time seemed to stand still. It was surreal, sitting across from these two gentlemen who knew each other. Both of them were handsome young men, and yet they were as opposite as you could get. Sam had light hair and a short, styled, polished haircut that made him look like he would play some sort of fancy sport like rugby, lacrosse, or tennis.

Sam was handsome, young, and athletic, and he was the better choice as a date since things with Ozzy were more complicated. Ozzy didn't look like a tennis player. He had on black jeans and boots and a T-shirt that was too tight. It was grey, and it had a graphic design of a monkey holding a Polaroid camera. His dark, curly hair was damp and he was holding a duffel bag, which was currently under the table touching my ankle.

I was undone by Ozzy. He had some brutish jealous masculinity simmering, and it made my bones warm. He had changed so much since I saw him last that I got lost staring at his physical features as he spoke slowly.

"...the end... of the world... if you can't make it," he finished his statement, regarding me with a serious expression.

"Oh, yeah, for sure I can make it," I said. "I'd love to see you while you're in town. Did you say you needed my help with something?"

"Yes. Please." Ozzy stood up abruptly. "Okay, so, I'll leave you two at it, but text me and we'll figure out a place to meet up some time while I'm here." Ozzy patted the table twice. "Samuel, good seeing you."

"Same," Sam said. "Maybe I'll see you again if you're here for a few days. Are you going to Dave and Alec's show?"

"Yeah. That's pretty much why I came in."

"Oh, are you playing bass with them?"

Ozzy shook his head. "Taking pictures," he said. "All right, well, I'll see you there," Sam said.

He barely had time to get the words out because Ozzy was taking off toward the door. He waved at us, making eye contact with me, only for the briefest of seconds before turning to walk away.

He didn't say anything to me. He seemed agitated, and I felt angry because of it. I remember the sight of that woman stretched out across the foot of his bed, and I could feel heat rise to my cheeks.

"I'll be right back, too," I said, even though I was the only one who would be right back. "I'm going to use the restroom real quick," I said, standing from my place at the booth and acting as normal as possible.

Concentrating on my new mission of using the restroom helped my flushed cheeks go back to normal.

My trip to the bathroom was quick and it felt like a whirlwind. All I did was wash my hands and even that didn't need to happen. I stared at myself in the mirror, wondering why I had trouble holding it together during one little interaction with Ozzy.

I washed my hands thoroughly and dried them, and even then, it felt like I was only in the restroom for a few seconds. I went back into the diner to finish things up with Sam.

He was such a good-looking guy. Some women would have definitely chosen him over Ozzy, but goodness.

Okay.

I needed to quit thinking about Ozzy.

I felt bad for feeling so drawn to him, and it was for that reason that I was extra nice to Sam when we parted ways. I told him I needed to leave, but it took ten minutes for us to walk to the car and say goodbye, and in the process, we exchanged contact information.

I was happy to meet Evelyn's friends and all of their children and grandchildren. I felt like I could actually call them if I needed something. This attribute was rare to find, but I had met some really nice people in Galveston, and Sam King was now on that list.

CHAPTER 7

Carl and Evelyn had a dog, a doodle dog of some sort that was black and white with fluffy spots. Her name was Lilly, and she was the cutest dog ever and accustomed to getting lots of love and affection. Lilly was always game for snuggling, and I loved it when Evelyn and Carl weren't home because she would hang out in my room.

Her curly fur was at least four inches long, and I sat on my bed and buried my fingers into it, wiggling them into the thick curls.

"You look like a killer whale had a baby with a cloud," I said. "I'm sorry, I'm sorry," I added in a singsong voice. "I don't mean that. Your mom was a poodle and your dad was a… I don't know what he was. A sheepdog? Are you half a sheepdog, Lilly?"

She wiggled excitedly. She loved it that I was talking to her. My words were basically gibberish because I could not get my mind off of one thing and that was… *Ozzy*.

"Now? Do you think I should text him now?" I asked out loud to the dog.

Lilly tilted her head at me like I was offering something good.

"I was just talking about texting someone," I said in a monotone voice that said she shouldn't get excited.

I had been sitting on the end of my bed, bent over, petting Lilly, who was on the floor. But I patted the end of the bed, and she jumped up there with me. My phone was close by, and I found it and went to the screen to text Ozzy. He had been the last to text me. Three times.

I rubbed Lilly a bit more before putting my thumbs on the keyboard.

Me: Hey. It was great seeing you, Ozzy. You look great. Your travels look good on you. Text back if you'd like to make plans to meet up again. I have a flexible summer schedule.

It had only been less than a minute when my phone dinged and I heard from Ozzy.

Ozzy: I wanted to take your picture. But it's not a big deal. It's just a personal project. It's no big deal if we can't find a time to connect.

Me: I thought that was why we were texting... to find a time to connect.

Ozzy: I'll be at The Supernova for that show on Saturday. If we don't hook up before, maybe I can run into you there.

Me: Oh, okay. I thought we were making time for it between now and then. But I'll go there if it's better for you.

Ozzy: Okay. Thanks.

That was all it said. I stared at it, and my heart felt broken.

I left it alone for a few minutes, more than five, less than ten, while I rubbed on Lilly absentmindedly and gave in to the miserable feeling of Ozzy being distant with me.

It felt somehow like my fault, which was ludicrous.

I texted him back.

Me: I would have been a better friend, Ozzy, and texted you back, but I felt bad contacting you after I talked to your girlfriend, Jasmine. I didn't want to interfere. It was still great seeing you today.

I pressed send after barely proofreading it. I was upset, and I knew you should never send texts when you're upset, but I did anyway.

Ozzy called me right back, and I wasn't expecting it.

I answered with, "Hello?"

"What are you talking about?" Ozzy asked. His tone was impassive, and I flexed my fingers, gripping a handful of curly hair on the dog's back.

"Your girlfriend," I said breathlessly. My mouth was dry. "Jasmine."

"Jasmine is not my girlfriend. I don't know who told you she was."

"She did," I said. "I called you on the phone one day and she called me back. Facetimed me, actually. From your phone."

"What? When? When was it?"

"It was right before you took that trip to Carolina to work with Logan Richie's family."

"I knew you started ignoring me when I went over there. You should have asked me, Evie. I would have told you the truth. I can't believe she did that, and I can't believe you believed it. You should have just asked me."

"You sound mad."

"I am mad," Ozzy said. "That's frustrating. I can't get in touch with you and then my cousin comes over to the gym, talking about how she just saw Samuel over at Carson's with Evie Taylor."

"That's all Gemma's doing. She met me there for lunch, Sam too, and then had to take off."

"Evelyn set you up with my cousin?"

"She's just trying to help me meet people. You remember, she was the one who introduced me to Bri and Caroline. And, by the way, I believe you about that girl, but just so you know, she was all sprawled out on your bed, looking mischievous and talking on your phone."

"Mischievous?"

"Promiscuous is maybe a better word. She seemed comfortable on your bed."

"That's because I've been friends with her for a year. Longer. Did you say she *called* you? Or did she pick up my phone? You know what, it doesn't matter. Either one is not okay. Look, I'm sorry that happened, but I don't have anything to hide."

"So, she's not your girlfriend? Have you ever kissed her?" I asked.

"Wu-n-no, I've, we've kissed, a couple of... a long time ago... but it's, it was her who kissed me. I've never kissed her, and we've certainly never said anything about being in a relationship. I would not hesitate to get a girlfriend and introduce her to Jasmine. I don't owe Jasmine an explanation about who I hang out with. Never have."

"Oh, well I wasn't saying I expected anything from you either. I just didn't want to interfere with you and someone else."

"Well, now you know you're not interfering."

"Okay," I said, smiling. "That's amazing. Thank you."

"So, can I take your picture, please?"

"Yes, your project."

"It's not a project," Ozzy said. "I took a photograph of you in your ballet costume that day. It's one I haven't shown you. It's my best work, and I'm just sort of, chasing that. I have an idea with a similar pose but slightly different lighting. But honestly it depends on the moment. I don't know if I'll be able to capture that exact expression again. I'd like to try."

"Did you say you have a photo of me you haven't shown me?" I asked.

"Yes," Ozzy said. "That's normal for me, but normally I keep photos from a client because I *don't* like them not because I do."

"I'll take that as a compliment," I said.

"It is one."

"That costume is gorgeous."

"The costume isn't in it."

"What?" I asked.

"It's just your face."

"Oh," I said.

"Artistically, you have a really interesting face, Evie."

"Oh. Thank you."

There were a few seconds of silence before I spoke again.

"So, am I still just seeing you at the show Saturday night?"

"Are you going to that show?"

"I was going to try to make it," I said.

"I figure we could hang out before that," Ozzy said. "I'm getting together with those guys tonight at band practice."

"Are you playing bass?"

"No. They're putting together a music video for one of the songs. We're getting footage from this weekend's gig, and they want me to video them some at Aiden's house, too."

"Thank you, but I'd be in the way for that," I said.

"No, you wouldn't. It'd be like old times."

"Yeah, but you're not playing bass this time. You're taking pictures. And I don't need to be in any of them."

"Just come, Evie," he said, giving me a hard time.

"Okay," I said since I couldn't refuse him.

"Fine. I'll pick you up at Evelyn's house at six o'clock. Band practice is at eight."

"You think there will be that much traffic?" I asked, sounding serious but playing around.

"We'll go eat first," he said.

"Where?" I asked.

"Elliot's, Miller's, The Spot, Waffle House, I don't care."

"Do you have access to a vehicle?" I asked. "Or should I pick you up?"

"I'll pick you up," Ozzy said. "I'll see you at six."

"Okay." I hung up the phone, and I immediately started straightening my room.

I lived in a guest room that was close to a side entrance of Gemma's house. I knew Ozzy would come to that door when he picked me up, so my first move was to clean my room.

Ozzy showed up at six o'clock exactly. I was looking out for him, and I stood at the door to wait while he walked up. He was wearing the same clothes he had on at Carson's earlier—black jeans and a tight grey graphic t-shirt. I was still wearing shorts, but I had changed into a t-shirt that said *Split Decision* across the front.

"Where did you get that shirt?" he asked.

It was the name of David and Alec's band. It was also a boxing term, but Ozzy knew it was one of their band shirts.

"Gemma had it," I said, looking down at my own shirt. "I think she bought it to support your brothers. She pulled it out when I said I was going to watch them rehearse tonight." I made a face of doubt. "Is it too much?" I asked.

71

"No, they'll love that," he said.

I gestured for Ozzy to come inside, and he followed me. I could not stop looking at him. He was still what you would consider to be a thin guy, but he looked way more substantial—more of a physical presence than he used to be. It was easy to be starstruck by Ozzy, and I had to remind myself that this was the same easygoing guy I had gotten to know for months. He looked different now, though. He hesitated by my door, and looked at me as if wondering where we were going.

"I figured we'd tell Gemma and Carl we were leaving," I said with a flick of my head toward the living room.

We headed that way and Lilly was the first to catch sight of us. She barked and barked until Ozzy stooped down to pet her. He spoke to her for a second, calming her down before standing again and focusing on Gemma who had now come up to us. She apologized for Lilly as she reached in to hug Ozzy.

"Jenny's oldest," she said. "Ozzy. How are you sweetheart?" There was an element of surprise in her voice.

But Ozzy just said, "I'm fine, how are you?"

"Doing good, Carl and I are both doing well. How about you?"

"I'm great. I'm still in Seattle, but I'm visiting for a few days."

"I see that. I was expecting Samuel," Gemma said explaining her surprise. "Evie told me she was going to see Jenny's boys' band, and I just assumed she was going with Samuel since they had lunch today. I didn't know she was going with one of Jenny's *actual* boys." Gemma was seriously surprised, but she looked pleased to see Ozzy. "Would you like to eat?" she asked. "Carl and I already ate, but we have all kinds of stuff in the refrigerator. Have you eaten? I have some things to throw together. Maybe make a little appetizer plate—some cheese and crackers. I think Carl has some prosciutto in there."

Gemma loved to entertain, and she smiled so hopefully that we both knew she really wanted us to stay and eat. I honestly didn't care either way, so I looked at Ozzy.

"You don't have to," Gemma said.

"No, I don't mind," Ozzy said. "We don't have any plans until eight o'clock, other than getting food."

"I can help you with the food part," Gemma said.

Ozzy looked at me and I said, "I'm fine with it. I was going to eat here before we talked."

My grandmother went to work like it was all decided. She washed her hands and instantly started looking in the refrigerator.

"Can I help with anything?" Ozzy asked.

"No, I'll just set a few things out on a plate for you two. Y'all just have a seat right here, or go in the living room, or whatever you want to do. I'll only be about five minutes."

Ozzy and I sat at the table while my grandma made a spread of cheeses, meats, and crackers. She was searching for one more item to add to the mix, and she agonized over what to choose, but she ended up scooping out some pear chutney.

I sat next to Ozzy at the table so that we could share the plate. Gemma sat on the other side of the table, and we stayed there for an hour, eating and talking. Gemma was fascinated by Ozzy's work, and she asked him all sorts of questions about his travels which led to him showing us some of the photographs he had saved on his phone.

He was amazing. It wasn't every day you met someone who was really skilled at something in life, and Ozzy was a profoundly talented photographer. Rarely did photographs make me feel things, but all of Ozzy's did. I knew he was good, but seeing his pictures and talking so openly about his work made me feel a little nervous around him.

He and Gemma talked about the photo shoot he did with Valerie and me, and she mentioned the framed print that was hanging in the living room. He hadn't seen it framed, and she promised to show it to him on our way out.

We had been sitting there for a while when the backside of Ozzy's hand found the side of my leg under the table. I looked at Gemma to see if she could see what was going on, but I didn't think she could. He was pretending to scratch the side of his own leg, but his hand touched me, and he left it there for several seconds. I was gut-wrenchingly attracted to this man. His touch sent waves of some type of expectant feeling coursing through me. My blood felt like warm honey.

I pulled away just enough that we lost contact.

I didn't want myself to want Ozzy so badly, but it was uncontrollable.

"Mac and Justin are coming to the show this weekend," Ozzy said to my grandmother, stating a random fact as he moved his leg, causing his hand to bump against me again.

"Oh, really?" Gemma asked. "Everybody will be excited about that."

"Yeah, I know," Ozzy said.

He moved his hand, letting his pinky hit my leg a little more securely than it had been before.

Blood was pumping through my veins, but Ozzy just went on talking like nothing at all was happening under the table.

"My brothers are all excited about how many people are going to be there. The band has really only been together for a year, and they sound solid. I think they have about twenty originals and a few covers."

"How many people in the band?" she asked.

"Four."

"And they've only been together a year?"

Ozzy nodded. "My brothers are driving the whole thing, though, and they've been playing and writing music together for years."

"Oh well, that sounds like fun," Evelyn said. "What's the location of the performance?"

"The Supernova," Ozzy said. "Down on the seawall."

CHAPTER 8

"Your photos have a way of making you feel things," I said a little while later when we were leaving Gemma and Carl's.

We were in his dad's truck, driving now, but we had just looked at the framed ballerina photo in Gemma's living room, so it was on my mind.

"All of them," I said. "Every single picture you take. They're all so interesting."

"Thank you, but like I was saying, I only keep and edit the ones I like. There have been thousands and thousands of dud photos taken that just get deleted."

"What'd you like so much about the one of my face?" I asked.

Ozzy smiled at me. "Your expression," he said. "You're pretty, too, and everything. The beauty is good, but it's more about the expression. I knew I was going to get the one I wanted that day."

His arm was on the console, but I didn't lean in or go anywhere near it. I just looked at it. His arms were noticeably different than they were at Christmas. Bigger.

"Ozzy, you've got muscles."

"I didn't mean to," he said with an easy smile. "I just enjoy doing that training. I don't know why it took me till now to figure it out. I should have started at Uncle Billy's gym years ago. I wasted a lot of time not doing that."

"Do you get hurt?" I asked. "Because your arm is bruised right there."

He looked down.

"It's on the inside. I noticed it at Evelyn's."

Ozzy was driving slowly, and he looked down at the bruise I was referring to.

"Oh, that's nothing. It's just a little surface bruise. It's from someone's fingertips—from them holding onto my arm right there."

"And that's nor-mal?"

"Yeah, kind of," he said toughly, smiling at me for being so tentative sounding about it. "It's just a little bruise. I don't even notice it."

"I'm sorry Gemma kept us so long," I said.

"It was fine," he said. "I didn't care what we did for dinner, and that tasted good."

"Well, thank you for staying," I said. "She lives for an impromptu buffet."

"I like Ms. Evelyn," he said sweetly. "Hey, do you mind if we go by my parents' house before we go to the rehearsal?"

"I'm up for anything," I said. "I knew we were running early. I was going to see if you wanted to get something else to eat since we didn't eat a huge dinner."

"It was plenty," Ozzy said. "Unless you're hungry."

"I was already full when she got out that banana bread."

"Me too," Ozzy said.

"Yeah, Carl's always been a picky eater, so Evelyn likes to feed other people."

"My family's like that, too. Uncle Billy cooks all the time, and his son, Will, is married to the woman who owns Elliot's."

"I knew that place was connected to your family," I said. "I forgot who told me. I've been there and it's really good."

Ozzy nodded. "Yeah, I'm never hungry when I'm in Galveston. Your grandma knows her way around the kitchen, though. I wouldn't turn that meal down if she offered it again. I got to hang out with Lilly, too."

"Yeah, Lilly's amazing. Gemma had to be on a waiting list to get her. She's a labradoodle, but that color is kind of rare. I tell her she looks like a sheepdog."

"She does," Ozzy agreed, but he was distracted because we were pulling into his parents' driveway. His mother was standing outside, watering the flowers, and she waved at us when she saw us pull up. I had been to this house before, and I felt comfortable here. Ms. Jenny was a cool lady.

"Hey, I thought you were going to Aiden's," Jenny said as soon as Ozzy opened the driver's door.

"I am. We are. Evie's with me. We're going there as soon as we leave here."

"Hey Evie Taylor," Jenny said as I got out of the other side of the truck.

"Hi, Ms. Jenny."

"I just wanted to show Evie some stuff on my computer."

"That's fine, babe, Dad's got the griddle on. He's making some quesadillas for dinner if y'all are hungry."

"Thanks," Ozzy said.

Jenny had a lot of flowers to water so she stayed put and we walked over there to greet her. We both gave her a hug on our way inside.

We talked to Ozzy's dad for a minute before making our way back to his room. Ozzy excused the state of affairs in his bedroom and said his mom used it as her craft room since he'd been living out of the house. It was true. It didn't even look like a bedroom. It was packed full of art supplies. There was a daybed in the corner and Ozzy's things were stacked neatly on one side of it, but that was the only sign of it being a bedroom.

Ozzy sat on the bed and opened his laptop. I had no idea what he was doing. I assumed he was looking for a photograph. I just stood there, glancing around, taking everything in as I waited for him.

"Oh, your hat," I said, noticing the black felt hat he bought last Christmas. It was sitting on a high shelf.

Ozzy glanced up there. "Oh, yeah."

"You left it?" I asked.

"Yeah. I didn't feel like wearing it on the plane, and it's kind of hard to pack. I have to keep my stuff to a minimum because of all my equipment. Sometimes my mom ships stuff, but I just put that up there and forgot about it."

"Can I get it down?" I asked.

"Sure," he said.

He didn't care at all. He was distracted with finding something on his computer. I reached up for the hat and pulled it down to inspect it.

It basically invited me to put it on.

I had seen Ozzy wearing it, and I had never felt tempted to try it on, but today was different. I turned it and placed it on my own head. There was a dresser and mirror close by and I walked over to it.

The design of my t-shirt had an 80's vibe to it and the hat complimented it. I took a second to tuck my hair behind my ears and adjust the hat where it sat just right on my head.

I turned to look at Ozzy, and he noticed the movement and glanced my way. I posed. It was completely impromptu and it came out a little like a frilly karate pose. I was confident, anyway, because I loved the hat and knew it matched my outfit.

"See? You," he said.

"What?" I asked, straightening up and looking at him.

Ozzy set his laptop next to him and stood up. He held his hands in L shapes and formed that stereotypical photographer's frame, viewing me from the other side of it. He put his hands down and looked straight at me as he came my way.

"That's the thing with you," he said. "Most of the time, I see something, a person, a scene, and I know I can capture it and manipulate it and make it even better than it actually is in real life. But with you, I can't. Even the photos I'm about to show you—they aren't as good as you were in person. That's why I wanted so badly to photograph you again. With everything else, I feel like I can make it better, but with you, I almost lose something."

He walked around me, studying me, looking at me curiously. It almost felt as though he was stalking me like prey, but he wasn't, he was genuinely curious, interested. He leaned toward me and breathed in. "Maybe it's just the whole experience that you lose," he said. "It's your smell, too, that adds to it. Also, there's this layer of positivity that just happens around you and I can't get it to translate to the camera. I almost did last time. That's what I was hoping to try for again." He was speaking slowly, softly, and seriously as he stood near me. He moved carefully, shifting slowly taking me in. He ducked and looked at me from under the hat. His face was only a few inches from mine.

"The smell is part of it, too, and that can't be conveyed in a photograph, unfortunately. It's a whole experience, being next to you, Evie." He hesitated for several seconds before he dazedly added, "...from a photographer's standpoint."

"Oh, because it's also an experience standing next to you, Ozzy, and I'm not a photographer," I said, causing him to smile.

That wolfish grin.

He was so irresistible that I changed the subject.

"Here, you try it on," I said, taking off the hat. I leaned back so that I could offer it to him. Ozzy smiled a little as he turned the hat and positioned it on his head. I could not stop a grin from spreading across my face. "You look so good in that," I said. "I'm surprised you left it here."

"Good enough that you'll let me kiss you?" he asked. His tone was so unaffected that I wasn't sure I heard him correctly.

"Huh? What?"

"Do I look good enough in this hat that I could kiss you right now and you'd let me?"

His straightforward question caused a warm sensation to happen in the innermost parts of my body. My body definitely reacted to this man. I felt an exciting, tingly sort of adrenaline flowing. My resolve threatened to crumble. I wanted to thrust myself into his arms. I wanted to kiss him so badly that I shivered with the effort to refrain from it. We just stood there for a few seconds, so close that I took note of his body heat.

"Evie," he said. His voice was soft, but it sounded like a low, hoarse rumble.

"Yeah?" I said without moving. Ozzy was wearing that hat, and I found it difficult to look at him without giving in to every urge in the book.

"Evie," he said again.

"What?"

"Look at me."

My eyes met his. It was difficult, but I did it. They were dark and even more piercing from under that hat. I held his gaze for as long as I could, which was just a second or two.

"You never did answer my question," he said. "And you keep looking away. Why are you doing that?"

"What was your question?"

"Would you let me kiss you, Evie?"

I was breathlessly desperate and I had no idea how I would get the words out. "I think I might... really wish you would do that righ—" I wasn't looking directly at him, so I didn't see when he started to duck and kiss me. I felt it happening, though, and I leaned tilting my head upward, eyes closed.

Fireworks.

Explosions.

I balled my hands into fists.

His mouth touched mine and I might as well have exploded into a million tiny bits. I was thrust into a hazy whirlwind where Ozzy's lips were on mine and nothing else happened— nothing else existed. We might as well have been shaken and stirred and become one person with how connected I was to him in that moment.

I felt his hand on my arm and didn't know when it got there. He used a light grip on my arm to pull me toward him, and I leaned his way, our lips connecting over and over. Ozzy's kiss was different than anything I had ever felt. He was gentle and tender, but he also seemed like he was completely in control. Maybe that's because I was putty in his hands.

"Thank you," he whispered, pulling back.

"For what?" I said.

He kissed me again, letting his mouth rest on mine for a few slow, sticky seconds before pulling back.

"For that," he said. "And this."

He kissed me again—it was tortuously slow and gentle, and I wholeheartedly enjoyed the act of standing there and letting it happen. I was more swept away by Ozzy than I knew was possible. These feelings were a surprise, and they left me reeling.

"Evie. Thank you."

He let go of me and gave me a smile. He took the hat off of his own head and put it on mine.

"My brother is coming," he said.

He took two steps away from me going back to his computer.

I heard footsteps coming down the hall.

"How'd you know?"

"I heard him yell for me," Ozzy said.

I hadn't heard that—not with all the toe-curling that had been happening.

I turned just in time to see David. The door was propped open and he just walked right in.

"What's up?" Ozzy said easily. "What are you doing over here?"

"We came to eat. Mom said y'all had quesadillas. Hey, Evie."

"Hey, David."

"I like that shirt," he said.

"Thanks."

"And that hat."

I smiled. "Thanks. It's Ozzy's."

"Oh yeah. Where'd you get that shirt."

"My grandma."

"You have one cool grandma," David said.

"What'd you need?" Ozzy asked.

"Oh, I was looking for you… Mom said you had Evie over here and I was making sure you were still planning on coming to Aiden's to video."

I knew I would be in the way. I told Ozzy I would be in the way.

"Yeah, I'm going. Evie's going with me."

"Oh, okay good," David said. "She should be in the video with that shirt on."

CHAPTER 9

Aiden was a little older than the rest of the band. He had a good job as a physical therapist. He had a nice garage and easygoing neighbors, so the band always held band practice at his house. He was also the band's drummer, and it was easier for him to avoid having to move his drum kit every time they rehearsed.

I was there at Christmas, and it was cool in his garage with a couch, chairs, and a rug off to one side, and the area where the band played over in the corner. It was a large, two-car garage, and Aiden parked his truck in there most of the time, but he moved it when the band was rehearsing, and the space felt open and inviting.

He had changed it some since the last time I was there. There were lights strung from the ceiling in a nice, even zig-zag pattern. He also added a dartboard and a couple of arcade games—a Pac-man game and a pinball machine. They were full size and fully operational, and Aiden had a jar of quarters set out to feed them. We hung out in there for a little while, waiting for Marc who was working and running late.

Alec called his girlfriend since I was there, and she came over. I could tell she felt some type of way about me having on a band t-shirt because she was staring at it from the moment she got there. Or it could have been the hat. She stared at me in general. But we adjusted to each other as quickly as possible and without the boys picking up on any awkwardness.

Her name was Natalie, and aside from the initial shock of seeing me in this t-shirt, we got along okay. Ozzy instructed Natalie and me to casually stand and silently play a game of darts together while the boys played the song. We did just that. We made a joke of trying to be actresses and look natural while casually playing a fake game of darts.

We whispered things to each other, making small talk. I told her I was an elementary school teacher, and she said she used to work at a daycare.

They played the same song about six times while Ozzy took a bunch of footage. The band would only get to play it once at the actual gig on Saturday night, so Ozzy wanted to have plenty of takes from the garage.

I interacted with Natalie and pretended not to watch Ozzy, but it was impossible for me. I loved the way he worked. I love watching him look at things—seeing his wheels turn as he calculated how to best capture a scene. I took glimpses of him anytime his camera wasn't aimed my way. I was in deep. I felt protective and maybe even a little possessive of Ozzy. One time I caught myself looking at Natalie and thinking that she better not be looking at him.

I knew Ozzy lived in Seattle and chances were slim that anything serious or long-term would happen between us, but I was so very smitten with him. Ozzy told the others we were leaving, and talked for a minute with them about the upcoming show. They thanked him and seemed really pumped about it.

"All right, we're heading out," he said.

Ozzy put his hand on my arm and I waved with my other arm so that I didn't have to break contact with him. It was the first time he had ever made physical contact with me in front of anyone else, and my heart pounded.

"Bye," I said. "You're sounding great. I'm excited about the show."

"Thank you," David said. "Bring your friends!"

Ozzy and I turned to leave, and his hand found me again, touching my back as we walked out. The contact was brief, but Ozzy was tender and caring toward me, and I wanted him so badly. I was aching to be next to him. I wanted to latch onto him like we were two lovebirds. It took all of my willpower not to do it.

"I took some pictures of you in there just now," he said, once we were in the truck.

"I thought you were videoing the band."

"How am I supposed to do that with you in the room?" He was being lighthearted. I knew he was focused on the video. I had been there and watched him work. But it gave me all sorts of feelings that he said he wanted to take pictures of me.

He smiled at me, and I did the unthinkable. I just reached out and put my hand in his.

89

I was sheltered in a lot of regards. I had a protective military father and I had not dated anyone long-term. I wasn't the type who needed or even wanted a boyfriend until I felt like I found the right person. I wasn't even sure, honestly, if Ozzy was that person.

The urge to hold his hand was literally more than I could handle, though, so I reached out and did it.

He did not skip a beat. He adjusted instantly, intertwining his fingers through mine and pulling my hand closer to him.

"Are you reaching out for me now?" he said. He was so sure of himself that it made me feel weak with desire. I acted confident, shrugging.

"A little," I said. "Is that so wrong?"

"No. I've been trying for months to get you to."

I smiled and squinted at him. "It's a little hard with you being halfway across the globe most of the time. I have to wait till you fly by my little piece of the world."

I made a gliding motion with my free hand, and Ozzy glanced at me and proceeded to stop the vehicle. He did it so abruptly that I gasped. Aiden lived in a newly developed neighborhood, and Ozzy quickly pulled into the driveway of a home that was still under construction. It was after 9pm, and nothing was happening. It was dark and deserted, and Ozzy parked in the driveway like he owned the half-built place.

He put the truck in park but left it running.

There was music playing on the radio, but I didn't pay attention to it because Ozzy kissed me. He leaned over the console and smiled at me briefly before kissing me. I went to him and there was no awkwardness or hesitation. My hat tilted back and I reached up and flipped it behind me, not caring where it landed.

Our mouths connected time after time, kissing each other slowly but non-stop. We did that what must have been ten times. His mouth was warm and perfect.

"Oh, goodness, Ozzy," I whispered. I spoke his name in such a hoarse whisper that he leaned in and kissed me with his mouth open. I opened mine to him, and he kissed me with his tongue. I felt the warm silk intrusion, and I was so lost in it that I let out a little moan when he pulled back.

He kissed me again when I did that, and for the next hour, we sat in that truck and kissed each other. We didn't say much, we just kissed.

Granted, that sounds like a long time but somehow, when it was Ozzy's mouth I was kissing, there was no such thing as time. I didn't even know what time it was until a little while later when we backed out of the borrowed driveway and I looked at the clock on the dash.

We went to the beach after that and walked for hours—until the middle of the night. We held hands and talked and walked. We would stop walking and stand in one spot for ten minutes and just hold each other and stare at each other.

When people on dating shows say if they like *long walks on the beach*, this was what they were talking about. This walk was the stuff of fairytales. Ozzy held me in his arms and the salty air moved fluidly around us, gently in every direction. It was wonderful. The sound of the waves and the feel of the sand, and Ozzy.

For hours that night, it was just me and the beach and Ozzy. He showed me how to hold my hands up and stand in a boxing stance. I was terrible at it, but I pretended to be confident and comfortable. Ozzy came up behind me to give me tips, but really, I wasn't paying attention to the boxing lesson with how on fire my body was where he touched it.

We were playful yet inseparable, and I was thankful for the empty beach and the cover of darkness. We were out there until two o'clock that morning. Afterward, he dropped me off at Gemma and Carl's, and we sat in their driveway for another hour. Even then, I wasn't tired, but I made myself go inside.

I was walking on clouds. It was the smack-dab middle of the night when I made it to my room. It was so late, it felt like morning. I considered staying up, which was just proof of how delirious I was.

I dug through my purse and found my phone for the first time all night. I had a few texts, including one from my mother. It hadn't been that long since I moved to Galveston, so she still called and got in touch with me quite a bit to see how I was making it. Sometimes she would text Bible verses, and tonight was one of those nights.

Mom: The grass withers, the flower fades, but the word of our God stands forever. Isaiah 40:8

I love you, Evie, and I'm so thankful. You've always had such a grasp on this verse with the way you draw near to God and keep Him in your life. I thought of you when I saw it. I'm so proud of you. Love, Mom.

I smiled at the way she signed off even though it was a text. I knew I couldn't text her back this late, but I read her text again.

And then something hit me.

That verse about the grass withering brought me back to the time I got saved. I felt those feelings of just knowing how great God's kingdom was and how small I was compared to it. And tonight, that verse hit me again. I vaguely remembered there being another verse that talked about God's word being sharp, like a sword, and cutting to the intentions of the heart. I felt that right then.

In those moments, I understood that if I were to ever have a relationship with a man with any sort of hope for longevity, it would have to be built upon and centered around faith in God.

It broke my heart, because instantly I realized that things weren't like that with Ozzy.

Things were backward. I liked Ozzy so much and I didn't want to talk about God for fear that it would make him uncomfortable around me. We had dozens of really deep conversations, and I still hadn't asked him how he felt about God. I felt convicted and heartbroken, and I cried about that.

I gave myself the night to sleep on it, but I contacted him the next morning when I woke up.

It was 11am. It was Friday and he would leave Sunday morning. We had plans to spend the weekend together, and it broke my heart but I knew I had to break them.

There was a text from Ozzy, and I called him back without giving myself time to fully wake up. I asked him to come over, and he agreed. He showed up on my doorstep fifteen minutes later. I opened the door, and he was standing there, looking fresh in dark jeans and a faded t-shirt. He smiled and stepped forward to hug me. I hugged him lightly but with nowhere near the same lack of caution that I was using the night before.

"Are you okay?" he asked when I reacted that way.

"I am, and I'm not," I said.

"What's that mean?"

"I was restless last night. I just had this whole, big, long thought process about God when my mom sent me a Bible verse in a text last night, and it made me realize, or remember, or whatever you want to call it, that I could go through all of life without ever even remembering to seek God. And if I did that, I'd really regret it."

"Okay?" Ozzy said. He spoke slowly, hesitantly.

"I've just got to… when I'm with you, I'm all wrapped up. I'm distracted. I know I like *everything* about you, Ozzy. I know your shoe size and your childhood fears, and I've never even asked how you feel about God. I feel really bad about that." A silent, hot tear came out of my eye and ran down my cheek.

"I didn't say you shouldn't love God," he said, seeing me cry. "I like that about you, Evie. You think I can't tell that you love God? Of course I can tell."

"Yeah, but you being okay with it is different than us building a life around... " I hesitated and let out a long, exasperated breath. "I don't know what I'm saying, Ozzy. I wish I could help you understand it. It's not anything you did wrong."

"But what? Are you saying you don't want to see me anymore? Because I never said I have anything against God, Evie."

"I didn't say that, and I don't know what I'm saying. I just need a minute," I said. "When I'm with you, it's just, I'm just so all-in, so consumed by this attraction, that it scares me. Just, please, Ozzy, give me a second to process these feelings and talk to God."

CHAPTER 10

*O*zzy stayed over for about fifteen minutes that morning. We had plans to spend the day together, but I called it off. If I spent the entire weekend with Ozzy it would end in something crazy like us eloping, or even more extreme, me giving myself to him without eloping. He was irresistible enough that I had to regroup and make a plan. I wasn't sure how much I could expose myself to him without falling in love, and I wasn't sure if it was smart to fall in love with someone like Ozzy.

That verse made me think about the shortness of life itself and the importance of centering my existence as much as possible around the Kingdom. I already liked Ozzy so much that I knew it was wise to take a breather and ask God if he was the one.

Ozzy texted me Friday night.

Ozzy: I'll wait, Evie. I'm not giving up. Take your time and pray or think or whatever you need to do, but nothing has changed for me. I'll be your friend at first if that's what you need. I'll come visit you and show you how to box. We can meet at the gym. No pressure. No rush. I like you, Evie. And I like God, too, if that counts for anything. I know we already said goodbye until next time, but I would love to see you again if you decide you want to.

I took a few minutes to think about it and then I texted him back.

Me: Thank you, Ozzy. I like you too. So much. Thank you for being patient. I'll let you know.

I had this whole other bit about boxing lessons and seeing him next time he was in town, but I deleted it and left it at that first part.

I didn't know whether or not I was doing the right thing. I wanted him so badly that it felt terrible and wrong to distance myself.

I had chores to do Saturday and a few errands to run that afternoon. I picked up my Bible and read it like eight different times that day, but nothing spoke to me. I wanted to agree to getting to know Ozzy as friends, but deep down, I knew that wasn't possible. I got a text that afternoon, and I thought it was Ozzy texting me back, but it was Sam King.

Sam: I was just checking to see if you're going to the Split Decision show tonight.

I didn't text him back right away. His text presented me with a question, which also gave me feelings.

The first thing I felt was the desire to go to the show. I did not want to miss the scene at the concert and I didn't want to miss the actual music. Most of all, I didn't want to miss Ozzy.

Seeing Sam's text made me feel fiercely loyal to Ozzy.

I prayed right then. I prayed for strength and most of all for an answer. I wish I could say I heard from God, but at that point, all I felt for certain was the overwhelming urge to be with Ozzy—to get my body next to his.

I needed to hear from God, though.

I had to know Ozzy was the one before I saw him again.

It was at that moment that I heard Gemma and Carl coming into the kitchen. I went in there and had to do a double-take because Gemma had on a hat that looked just like Ozzy's.

"We just came from the farmer's market," she said.

I knew the hat guy was usually there, so I assumed she bought one that looked just like Ozzy's.

"I ran into your Ozzy, and he gave this to me to give to you. He had it on and I complimented him. He took it off and gave it to me—said it was yours, anyway—said you left it in his truck."

Gemma came to stand in front of me. She was in her seventies, and she still made a playful little pose as she took it off of her own head and presented it to me.

"I figured you'd wear it to the show tonight."

"Oh, the show? I didn't think I was planning on going."

"Why ever not?" she asked, stopping in her tracks and looking thoroughly confused.

"Because I—"

"Because that boy seems like the one to me, Evie."

My heart pounded and tears sprang to my eyes. I blinked. Gemma never said things like that, for one, and two, she seemed serious.

"What?" I asked, trying to be lighthearted.

"You should probably see him before he leaves."

"Really?" I asked.

She nodded and smiled, staring me straight in the eyes. "Really," she said. "He's precious, Evie, and he loves you."

My heart pounded so fast it felt like it doubled up on itself and was going half-speed again. My jaw ached with the pain of unshed tears. I hugged her so that she wouldn't see my eyes watering.

"Thank you, Gemma," I said. I waved at Carl, who had just come in and had a few paper bags in his arms. "I'll be back in just one minute to see how you and Carl did at the market."

I had to calm myself down. I had looked into Gemma's eyes when she said Ozzy was the one, and I felt something surreal. I knew it was just my grandmother, but I felt like it was God talking to me. It felt like the exact confirmation I had been waiting on. I was shaken, and it felt like a dream for me to reach up and place Ozzy's hat on my head as I walked down the hall.

I went straight to my room—straight to the bottom drawer of my closet dresser.

That was where I kept a few random clothing pieces. They were brand new or seldom worn clothes and a few accessories, like scarves. I dug to the bottom of it—to a shirt I bought for myself before I moved to Texas. It was an 80's remake and it was a black, vintage-looking shirt that had the word Ozzy written across the front in a decorative logo-style font.

Ozzy was all it said. I tried it on, and put the hat on with it. I stood in front of the mirror only long enough to confirm that I was definitely going to the concert and I was definitely wearing this outfit.

I stripped it off instantly and put on my other shirt. I went back into the kitchen to meet Gemma and Carl. I smiled at the fact that my decision had been made just like that. I was going to the concert, and I was going there for Ozzy.

***

It was later that same evening when I got dressed to go to The Supernova. The doors opened at 8pm, but there were two opening bands scheduled to play before Split Decision went on.

I called, and the guy who answered said that David and Alec's band would start playing at 10:30 or 11. I got dressed in time to get to The Supernova by around 9, and it was already packed by the time I arrived.

I wore white jean capris and a fitted jean jacket with the sleeves rolled. I left it open in the front, clearly exposing my Ozzy t-shirt. I wore white sandals and, of course, the hat. I loved the outfit, and I felt confident, but I began to feel a little exposed when I got there and saw how packed the place was. I smiled at myself for wearing a shirt with Ozzy's name and I felt self-conscious enough to close my jacket a little before I interacted with the guy at the door.

"Cool hat," he said, basically yelling over the loud music.

"Thank you," I replied.

I paid the cover charge to get in, and he stamped my hand and let me through.

"Evie!" It was a woman's voice, and I turned to find Bri who was walking while carrying a drink and a basket of French fries. "Oh, cool shirt, Ozzy would love that," she said, speaking loudly. "He's in town, right now. He's here tonight." She motioned with a flick of her head for me to follow her, and I did. "He's leaving tomorrow," she informed me casually as we walked.

I didn't want to think about it.

"Yeah," I said, simply agreeing.

The closer we got to the stage, the louder the music got, so she just turned and walked and I followed her. Bri turned once we made it to a partition near the soundboard.

She leaned in to speak to me. "I didn't even ask you if you wanted to come over here with me," she said. "You might be waiting on someone. But either way, I'm over there by the wall with my family. There's a bunch of us at those tables."

I looked in that direction, and I saw Ozzy standing next to Mac, Morgan, and a guy I had never met before. I recognized him as Justin Teague, Mac's teammate and Katie's husband. They were talking and not looking our way, and I was so nervous I could hardly breathe. Ozzy was wearing all black like he often did when he worked.

"Go ahead," I said to Bri before Ozzy had the chance to look my way. "I need to use the restroom. I'll meet you over there in just a second."

Bri smiled and nodded, and I turned and high-tailed it away from Ozzy and the group of his family and friends. There were famous people in the crowd. Mac's mom, and Billy Castro, and Justin—it was a star-studded side of the room. I was suddenly doubting the shirt. I was suddenly doubting everything.

I had never been in this venue before, but I headed to the back of the room where I assumed I'd find the restrooms. The lights were low, the music was loud, and I ducked and weaved through groups of people who were standing around, listening to the band. I didn't look at them long enough to see if I recognized anyone. I kept my head down, heading any way but toward Ozzy and the overwhelmingly cool group of people he was with.

I saw a hallway with a sign labeled *Restrooms*, and I went straight for it. I told myself I could always button my jean jacket if I chickened out about wearing the shirt in front of him.

There was an exit at the far end of the restroom's hallway, and I caught myself thinking about walking out of it instead of going to the restroom at all. I passed the restrooms and kept walking. The pulsing bass of the music was behind me and the exit sign was before me. I was overwhelmed by the thought of seeing Ozzy—surprising him, and I gave some serious thought to walking out of that door.

Then I felt a warm hand come around my upper arm. I hadn't seen or heard Ozzy approach, and I turned and was both relieved and stunned to see him.

"How'd you find me so—" but I couldn't finish my sentence because Ozzy pulled me into a hug. It was so fast and firm that my hat, his hat, the hat I was wearing fell off and landed on the floor behind me. I didn't care. I held onto Ozzy unrepentantly. I clutched onto him like I had done the other night at the beach.

CHAPTER 11

Ozzy held onto me, pressing me against him. His midsection was firm and tight, like a tree trunk, and I pressed the side of my face to his chest. He had on a thin black t-shirt and I could feel his body heat through it.

Suddenly, he moved, peeling me off of him, holding me by the arms and pushing me back so he could get a look at my shirt.

My heart p-p-pounded as he inspected the front of my shirt. He wore a serious expression. His eyes roamed from the front of my shirt slowly all the way up to meet my eyes again. He licked his lips absentmindedly as he checked me out, and I wanted to melt. His all-black outfit made him look dangerous. He was dangerous. He was staring straight at me in a noisy dark hallway and blood raced through my veins at breakneck speed. His face broke into a slow grin.

"Nice shirt," he said.

He was so slow, easy, and deadpan with his statement that I let out a laugh. "Thanks," I said.

His gaze held mine. He had a hold of me by my arms, and his eyes roamed to my shirt again. People came and went in and out of the restrooms, but we were far enough from the doors that we didn't pay attention to them.

"That's my name on your shirt," he said.

Our gazes held and I smiled and nodded. "Oh yeah?" I asked in a happy tone, trying to seem like I hadn't noticed. I acted unaffected even though my arms felt scorched in the places where he was touching me.

"Do you just like that guy's music, or…"

"Who? Ozzy Osbourne?" I asked. "No. I don't even, I've never… I don't even know what he sings. And now that I say that, I don't even know if he is a singer. He could just be the guitar player for a band."

"You don't know what the guy on your shirt does?"

"Well, I know he's a musician. Maybe from Kiss?"

He smiled. "My mom always told me that if I'm going to wear a t-shirt, I better be ready to answer questions about whatever is on it."

"So, is Ozzy not from Kiss?" I asked.

He shook his head, and I shrugged.

"Well, it's a good thing I'm not talking about that Ozzy when I wear this shirt."

"Hmm, interesting. What Ozzy are you talking about?" he asked.

He was about six inches taller than me, and his back was to the venue, blocking me so I couldn't see down the hallway.

"Ozzy, have you seen Ms.—" The male voice came from behind Ozzy but it broke off when he came close enough to notice me standing there. "Oh, hey... are you Ms. Evelyn's granddaughter?" Mac asked.

"Yes!" I said.

Ozzy and I let go of each other when Mac walked up. I remembered Mac from when I was a little kid and I beamed at him, noticing how he still looked the same. He was older than me, but he was a nice kid, and I had played with him more than a few times growing up.

"Evie?" he asked.

"Yes!" I said. "Hey, Mac!"

"Wow, you're all grown up, I can't believe it." He came in for a hug and I used the opportunity when we broke apart to reach down and get the hat off of the floor. He saw my shirt as I was standing up. "Cool shirt," he said, smiling at me. "Is that for this Ozzy or the other one?"

"This one," I said.

Mac smiled at that. "This is a good one."

"We were just talking about that, actually. I realized I had no idea what the other Ozzy actually did. This Ozzy told me he wasn't part of Kiss, but we never established what he *was* part of."

"I actually have no idea either," Mac said.

"He's a singer," Ozzy said. "He was in a band called Black Sabbath."

Mac nodded like that sounded familiar to him, but I just sucked air through my teeth, making a sound like I was rubbed the wrong way by that, which I was.

Ozzy gave me an amused grin. "I knew she would hate that," he said to Mac.

Mac laughed and reached out to hug me. "It's so good seeing you, Evie. I have such fond memories of your grandma. Please tell her that for me. I miss Ms. Evelyn. Bri said you were here, and I wanted to catch you. Are you sticking around? Are you sitting with us?"

I nodded. "Yeah, yeah, thank you. I'll come over to where you guys are if you don't mind." I knew Ozzy would be working, and I felt thankful for the invitation.

"Oh, great. We'll be out there. I'll talk to you some more. I just wanted to make sure you weren't leaving." He patted Ozzy on the shoulder and turned to head back to the main room, smiling at someone who was walking down the hall. I didn't bother checking it out. I stayed against the wall, under the cover of Ozzy whose chest was significantly broader than it was when we met.

He reached out and pulled me toward him using a hand on the back of my waist. The hat was between us, and he took it from me, holding it to the side so he could pull me closer. He held it near our faces, shielding us from any possible onlookers. There was a wall to my right and a hat on my left. Ozzy was right in front of me. I was in love.

"I thought you weren't coming," he said, holding onto me with one hand and the hat with the other.

"I wasn't but then I thought maybe God was... I got that hat and I just had to come."

"I knew I did right by giving Ms. Evelyn this hat," he said with a grin.

I leaned up and he kissed me for a long, glorious second. His mouth was firm and soft and perfect, and he kissed me twice and then a third time before pulling back far enough to focus on me.

"I'm so sorry I asked you to leave me alone," I said, speaking vulnerably. "I should have never done that. I know you weren't trying to rush me into anything. And I'm not trying to make things complicated or make it seem like I'm better than you, because I'm not. I'm just scared of how much I like you."

Ozzy smiled. "That's nothing you should be scared of. I just want you to give me a chance. There's no harm in giving me a chance." He turned, reaching back for me, pulling me with him as he took off down the hall. He leaned in toward me. "I need to go take some photos of the guys backstage, but there's room over there with my family," he said. "Please don't leave."

"I'll be fine," I promised. "Just go do what you need to do."

Ozzy handed me the hat, and I let go of his hand long enough to put it back on my head.

"Is my lipstick okay?"

He glanced at my mouth, but only for a split second before he stepped toward me, rushing me swiftly, kissing me like he just couldn't help himself.

"No," he said. "I didn't even know you had it on."

"I barely did," I said.

"Well, you don't at all anymore," he said.

He kissed me one last time just for good measure before taking off to work with his brother. He promised he'd be back for a little while during the break, but I told him I was fine and that he should take his time with his brothers.

His entire family was there and many of their friends, too. There must have been at least fifty of them. Mac was the first one I saw when I went over, and he introduced me to those who were standing close enough to talk to us.

The opening band was playing music, and all the people closest to the front were paying attention to them. Those of us who were waiting for David and Alec's band were around the edges of the room and positioned far enough from the band that we could speak to each other openly and not interrupt the band at all. I already knew Caroline and Bri, but everyone else in my immediate vicinity was new. I had never been to this place. It was loud and crowded, and if I were by myself, I would have hated it, but as it stood, it was fun.

Someone spotted it and asked about my shirt, and I told them I found it months ago and wore it tonight to mess with Ozzy Abramson. I had already thought about what I would say and how I would say it, and they laughed at my explanation and said they loved it just like I hoped they would.

I saw Sam from a few tables over, and he came over to me while I was still talking to Mac and Morgan. We talked for a minute and he asked if I'd like anything to eat or drink. I told him I was fine and thanked him.

Mac smiled at me after Sam walked away, and I didn't know what to say to him. "I never hear anybody call him Sam," he said.

I smiled. "Oh, that's funny. My grandma introduced him to me as Samuel, but he almost instantly told me his friends call him Sam."

"I had no idea," Mac said, shaking his head.

"Ozzy said that same thing," I said.

"Yeah, I hear a lot of people call him Sam," Caroline added, overhearing us.

I talked to them for twenty or thirty minutes before we were interrupted by the band thanking the audience for a great night and announcing that they were finished playing. Loud dance music began pumping out of the speakers as soon as they announced they were finished.

Mac's little brother, Andrew, had his girlfriend there with him. She heard that I was teaching at Crestview in the fall. She told me she was studying to be an elementary school teacher and that maybe we would be co-workers one day. She was really friendly, and I was smiling at her when I felt a tap on my shoulder.

It was Sam, and he nudged his chin at me. "Do you feel like dancing?" he asked. More people started to dance once the band stopped playing and rap music came on. Sam was extremely handsome and most girls would have jumped at the chance to take him up on that offer. I opened my mouth to make some excuse that I didn't know yet, but thankfully Mac saved me from having to think so quickly.

"I have a feeling Ozzy might strangle you with his bare hands if he heard you asking her," Mac said, looking over his shoulder at their cousin. "You know he can do that now, right?"

Sam looked confused for a second. "Oh, are you and Ozzy…"

"You didn't see her shirt?" Mac asked, smiling.

"What shirt?"

I turned toward Sam and he checked out the front of my shirt. I had my hands in the pockets of my jean jacket and I opened it a little.

"Is that about Ozzy Abramson?"

I nodded, and Sam, being the confident playboy that he was smiled really big and said, "Oh, snap," before smirking at me and walking away. He didn't mention us having lunch.

I watched him, and he had another girl on his arm by the time he reached the dancefloor. He just walked by someone, said a few words, and she followed him. I was grinning at the sight when Ozzy came up behind me.

"What are you smiling at?" he asked, tugging briefly at my jacket.

I turned to him. "Hey, I didn't even see you come from over there."

He came to stand next to me. I could smell all sorts of things in the room, but I got a faint whiff of Ozzy's cologne as he came near. It was clean and woodsy and I breathed it in as he came close enough to talk to me.

"We were outside for a minute, and Aiden's truck is on the street, so I came in through the front door."

I was about to respond to him, but Mac leaned over to speak to us. "I had to bulldog Samuel just now. He was over here trying to get Evie to go out there and dance with him."

Ozzy looked at Mac, then me, and then out at the dancefloor where Sam was currently dancing with a tall blonde. He wasn't all over her, but he wasn't being shy either. Ozzy started to say something, but he just shook his head a little and smiled.

And then something else caught Ozzy's eye. "Hang on," he said staring distractedly.

It was a photograph opportunity. This exact thing had happened several other times when we were hanging out. I knew that faraway look he got when he spotted something and needed to take a picture of it.

"I'm sorry, don't move, stay here, I love you, I'll be right back."

Ozzy spoke quickly and kissed my cheek after that rapid-fire sequence of words. And just like that, he took off through the crowd to photograph whatever caught his eye.

He had said *I love you*. Sure, he probably didn't even realize it. He was being lighthearted and apologizing for leaving me so abruptly.

But he said it.

CHAPTER 12

⟫⟫⟫—⟪⟪⟪

*O*zzy walked over to Billy and Tess.

They were standing against a wall, Tess's back to Billy's chest, swaying and listening to the music—looking like teenagers in spite of being grandparents.

They were adorable, and I wasn't surprised when I saw Ozzy go up to them. I took a step back to watch him in action.

There were people all around me. All of them were friendly and I could have struck up an instant conversation with any of them when Ozzy went away, but I was content to stand back and take everything in.

I watched Ozzy and I looked all around, hearing the heavy pulsing bass sound of the hip-hop music and taking in the sights and sounds all around me. David, Alec, and the band were on stage setting up their instruments and getting ready to play. I watched them for a minute before I saw Katie Teague headed my way. She was looking straight at me, so I prepared myself to talk to her.

115

"Aunt Laney asked me to come get you," she said. "That's Ozzy's grandma. She's over there by Aunt Jenny and them. She's got a foot brace on right now, or she would have come over here. She asked me to come get you… to see if you'd come over there and talk to her."

"Oh, sure," I said.

I spoke in an easy tone in spite of the wave of nerves that hit me at the thought. I had noticed their group before. It was my grandma's best friend, Ms. Abby, along with Laney Graham and Jenny and Sean Abramson, Ozzy's parents. Other people were over there, too—aunts and uncles, along with Cody, Audrey, and a few of the younger cousins.

I followed Katie behind two other tables to get to them. I was closer to Ozzy now, but he was still busy with Tess and Billy.

Mrs. Graham smiled and waved me over when she saw me approaching. Ozzy's mom was standing close by, and she stepped out and intercepted me before I could get to her mom. She hugged me and told me it was good to see me. She complimented me on my outfit, and I thanked her. I did my best to be in the moment, but I was nervous and had to concentrate my efforts on not shaking.

Katie went back to talking to her husband and I went to Ms. Laney who was sitting at a table, waiting for me. She motioned with a wave of her hand for me to come over and I walked that way. She stayed seated but opened her arms for me to come in for a hug.

"I just had foot surgery, or I'd get up," she said, close to my ear.

"Oh, that's okay. Ozzy was telling me about that. Did it go okay?"

"It did, thank you, baby. Hey, why don't you grab one of those chairs and sit down next to me for a minute? I don't want you to have to squat the whole time."

The chair in question was about ten feet away, and I was thankful for the chore so that I could catch my breath. I found the chair and carefully carried it through wall-to-wall people to the tiny piece of open space next to Mrs. Graham. The music was loud, so she leaned over to speak close to my ear so that she wouldn't have to yell.

"I'm sorry about not getting up," she said.

"Oh, don't worry about it, I was happy to sit down for a minute." I wasn't making eye contact with her since she was leaning over and talking next to my ear.

She smelled like my ninth-grade English teacher, and I figured they must have the same perfume. I was fond of that teacher, and I smiled as I leaned toward Ozzy's grandma, feeling comforted.

"A mother wants the best for her children," she said. "You'll see that one day when you become one." I glanced at her with a sincere smile because I hadn't expected her to say something so heartfelt. "The same goes for a grandmother with her grandchildren," she said. I turned to let her speak near my ear again. "I want all of my family to flourish and to have a good, abundant life. And, honestly, Evie, I know I sound like an old lady saying this, but God, our creator, is a big part of that. Jenny and Sean and all of their boys... they're such an amazing, artistic family. I'm so proud of them, but knowing God... that's what sets a mother's and grandmother's soul at ease." She paused and patted me, but I could tell she was going to continue. "I'm not going to tell you the whole story, sweetheart. Not right now at least. But Ozzy came to me yesterday, and we had a long talk about Jesus. Jenny was there, and, well, we talked more about that stuff than we had in years, honestly." She squeezed my arm. "I just wanted to thank you for that," she said. "I know it was something you said that sparked it all, and I just wanted to thank you for that."

"Oh, goodness, you're welcome," I said, not knowing what else to say. "I didn't do anything."

"Yes, you sure did," she said. "I can't remember a single time in my life when someone has come up to me asking if I knew a way they can get closer to God. It'd be great to have that conversation with anybody, but when it's your grandson, it is just more special than I can even tell you, Evie. I just thank you. I see your grandmother in your smile, and I see her goodness." She smiled and patted my hand. "But I didn't mean to get serious. I know you want to enjoy the show. I just know Ozzy's leaving in the morning, and I didn't know when I'd get the chance to see you again. I just wanted to thank you for causing Ozzy to think about things, sweetheart."

I had been feeling bad about being so hard-nosed with Ozzy, and here she was, thanking me. "You're so welcome," I repeated, not knowing what else to say.

I hugged her since we were leaning toward each other anyway. She leaned in to hug me.

"I saw some of Evelyn's photos of you and her other little granddaughter—the ones Ozzy took."

"Yes ma'am."

"Those were really pretty," she said.

"I think Ozzy makes things prettier than they appear in real life," I said, smiling. "That's why he gets paid the big bucks."

She laughed at that. "I love your outfit," she said. "That's so cute. I like that shirt."

When she started to say I like that, I assumed she would mention the hat. I started to thank her and say that it was Ozzy's, but I put a hand to my chest when she pointed out the shirt.

"I had no idea what band Ozzy Osbourne was in," I explained, since we had just had that whole conversation about the Lord.

"Oh, is that an Ozzy Osbourne shirt?" she asked. "I thought it was for my grandson."

"It actually is for your grandson," I said. "I mean, it was made for the other one, but when I bought it, I didn't know anything about that other guy. I didn't know what band he was in." I felt nervous about saying too much, and I added, "I thought this Ozzy would get a kick out of it."

"He looks like he did," she said. "And maybe he's trying to get a look at it. He's been taking pictures of us for a minute now."

I broke eye contact with her right when she said that. I looked toward Ozzy, and sure enough, his big lens was aimed right at me and he was standing behind it.

I made a face at the camera and at him, and I saw the shutter close several times before he put down the camera, smiling. In a practiced move, he put on the lens cap and dropped the camera to his side, shielding it with his hand as he walked.

He was coming toward me and I smiled at him. Mrs. Graham was looking at us. I could feel her watching me watch him approach, and I still sat there and stared at him, grinned at him.

He came around me and stooped between our chairs. "I see you found a chair," he said to me.

"I asked her to sit with me for a minute," his grandma said. "I'm stuck down here with my foot."

"Do you need to move to see David and Alec?"

"Oh, no, honey I can see fine from here. It's too loud over there, anyway. I was just saying that Evie probably doesn't want to be stuck sitting down."

"We don't mind," he said. "I'll be able to relax once I'm done getting footage, but I'm going to take Evie with me for now."

"Okay," she said easily. She and I hugged again before I got up.

Ozzy stood, pulling me with him. He held my hand as we made our way through the crowd.

He handed Mac his camera. "Guard it with your life," he said to him.

Mac seemed to take the request seriously. He nodded and instantly began strapping the camera around his neck. Ozzy didn't stick around to see what kind of job he did. He pulled me onto the dance floor, past Sam and the blonde, and into the center of the crowd.

People were having a good time. The music was loud, and they were into it. It was a medium-tempo hip-hop groove, and couples danced together. Ozzy pulled me into the middle of it, smiling as he reached a small opening on the dance floor.

It was dark, and everyone around us was moving and swaying and not looking at us. I went into Ozzy's arms, letting him lead me—move with me. He wrapped an arm around me, going between my shirt and my jacket. I could feel his body heat through the thin layer of my t-shirt. His arm flexed around me like an anaconda, and I felt weak in the knees as I leaned into him. Ozzy moved, swaying to the music. I was classically trained and could hold my own as a dancer, but Ozzy was really good at this. He grinned confidently as he moved, leading me. His timing was perfect, and he pulled me along with him.

He wasn't all over me, but he was at the same time. He was holding onto me, completely supporting me, dancing with me. I held him with a gentle grip. I ached to be near him. I got lost in the swaying—in the music. Ozzy held onto me, and I was lost in it.

The pulsing rhythm was so loud that there was a blanket of sound. The pounding of my heart was lost in the heavy beat, and I leaned into Ozzy letting myself sway with him. He held me close and we danced, moving in each other's arms.

I glanced to the side dazedly and saw Sam, Katie, Nick, and several other family members including a couple of uncles— Will, Evan, Lucy, the famous writer. I noticed these people vaguely, but everything always went back to Ozzy. He held me and moved, and one song morphed into another one, a slower one.

Ozzy held onto me. "May I have another dance?" he asked, still moving.

"Is that what this is because I didn't think we were…"

"Oh, I could always stop," Ozzy said. He stopped moving abruptly when he said the word, and it caused me to squeeze him and get him moving again.

"I was just saying that I didn't think you needed to check in with me about another dance. I just assumed we would do it again."

Ozzy adjusted me in his arms.

I wanted to say I assumed we'd never dance with anyone else, ever again. But I kept it to myself.

For a while—for what must have been fifteen seconds, Ozzy just held me and danced with me, saying nothing. "You, Evie," he said finally. "You. You. You. The shape of your face, and the proportions of your smile. I can't turn it off. I want to hold you and look at you. I want to sit on the couch with you and watch television and watch you watch television. And I really… I really want to kiss you. I want to do that right now."

He spoke so slowly that I felt like I might fall off some sort of cliff as I waited for him to finish all he wanted to say. I tried to remember to move—tried to remember to breathe. I moved to speak next to his ear again.

"I think you can do that whenever you like," I said.

I felt the side of his cheek flex as he listened to me and then stretched as he smiled at my words. He moved. I thought he was going to kiss me, but he held me, speaking to me again. "I'm barely keeping myself from doing it. The only reason I am is because I'm trying to be a gentleman with all my family here."

"Thank you," I said, even though I desperately wanted him to *not* be a gentleman.

I turned to his ear again. "I don't want this moment to end, Ozzy."

CHAPTER 13

"How is everybody doing out there, Gal-ve-ston?" A man came on stage and asked the question charismatically over the microphone at the same time that someone turned down the music.

I was on the dance floor with Ozzy and had been out there for a few songs when that happened, and Ozzy instantly took me by the hand and began walking. I knew he had to get to work, so I kept pace with him.

The guy went on talking to the crowd and announcing that the main act, Split Decision, was coming right out. He talked, and they kept responding. It was loud and everyone was focused on the stage, so Ozzy and I just weaved our way through them.

He stopped and turned to me when he got to Mac. He took his camera from Mac absentmindedly as he looked at me. "I'll be busy during the first few songs."

"Yes. Go. Take your time. Don't worry. I'll be over here."

Ozzy took off. I sat with Caroline and a whole group—Bri, Nick, Cody, Mac, Morgan, Katie… there were so many of us standing and sitting around in a section of high-top tables that I didn't recognize them all. I talked to the people right around me for a minute, but once the band started, we all paid attention to them.

They were really good, and I *tried* to watch them, but I kept finding Ozzy. He was focused on his work, and I loved seeing him move and interact with people. I was proud of him. I was a fan. Wearing the T-shirt with his name on it was an accurate reflection of my feelings. Ozzy was cool and smooth, and I tried not to watch him work, but I couldn't help but steal glimpses of him.

The first set passed, and I talked a little but watched mostly. I excused myself during the last song. It had been a while since a server came by, and I was thirsty. I went to the end of the bar, hoping to wait until the bartender had a minute. There were two people working the bar, and I caught the eye of the guy who was standing closest to me. He was the same person who had made the announcement earlier.

"Josiah Brown," he said coolly, pointing at me.

"Evie Taylor," I said, smiling and leaning over the bar to speak to him.

"Hi, Evie. I'm Colton."

"I thought you said it was Josiah Brown."

"I meant your hat," he said.

"Josiah Brown. That's who made it, right? He's my cousin's-husband's-dad."

I touched the hat. "It's borrowed," I said. "I'm not sure who made it."

"Believe it or not, not only do I know who made your hat, but I knew your name. I knew your name before you told me."

"How?"

"My sister is the assistant principal at Crestview. I saw your file sitting on her desk." He smiled and put a hand up in surrender like he knew that might be a creepy thing to say. "I promise I'm not a stalker or anything. I just have a good memory. I saw your file, and I knew you were Evie Taylor before I ever walked over here."

"Well that's kind of cool *and* weird," I said.

He laughed. He was a charismatic guy, and he leaned against the counter, drying a glass with a clean towel in the most bartender pose you could ever think of.

"I just have a good memory," he said. "There was also a Sheila Broussard and a Tyler Moss in that stack of new employees—a lunch lady and the new P.E. coach."

I smiled. I had met Tyler, the P.E. coach.

"I'm excited to work at Crestview," I said. "I've met your sister a couple of times, and she's really nice. I can actually see that you two look alike, now that I think about it."

He smiled. "Everyone says that. What can I get you to drink Evie Taylor?"

"Just some water, please."

"Water? That's all?"

"Sure."

Colton used the glass he had been drying, put some ice in it, and set it on the little tray in front of him. "Kindergarten, huh?"

"Yep."

"I saw you dancing with Ozzy Abramson. Are you two seeing each other?"

"I wish," I said shrugging with a little grin.

Colton smiled at me for saying that.

"Yeah, I was wondering because I knew he didn't live here. I know their family—David and Alec. I gave them the gig here tonight."

"Oh, are you the manager? This is a nice place."

"No, it's actually... thank you, but I own it."

"Oh, cool, wow, nice," I said, feeling surprised since he was so young.

"Thank you," he said. "I like it."

"Yeah, definitely. Well, hey, I'm sure I'll be seeing you around Crestview maybe. And in the meantime, what do I owe you for the water?"

Colton started looking behind me while I was talking. "What's up Ozzy?" he said. He stepped forward and reached out his hand just as he said that, and I turned to find Ozzy, who was coming up right beside me. It was crowded in there, and he came into my space as he leaned in to shake Colton's hand.

I grinned at him as he brushed up against me. There was to be a fifteen-minute set break starting now, so loud thumping rap music began playing again.

"Colton's sister is the vice-principal at Crestview," I explained speaking over the sound.

Ozzy nodded.

"And this is his place," I added.

"I know Colton," Ozzy said, still nodding.

"How long are you in town, Ozzy?"

"Just till tomorrow morning," Ozzy said. "I basically came in for this show."

Colton smiled and nudged his chin toward the stage. "So, you're taking a little breather?"

"I already have all the footage I need," Ozzy said. "It was good to see you though, Colton. Do we owe you anything for whatever Evie ordered?"

"No, no, it's just water. You're looking jacked, Ozzy. I thought you just put on a little weight, but then I realized it was muscle. You've been hitting the gym, huh?"

"Yeah, some MMA."

"Still up in Seattle?"

"Yep." He smiled at Colton before focusing his attention on me. "Hey, my mom and grandma and a whole group are heading out. I thought we'd go tell them goodbye."

"Oh yeah, hey, it was nice meeting you, Colton," I said, waving at him as we walked away.

I took a sip of the water as we walked since I was seriously thirsty and knew we were about to talk to people. We were about halfway to his family when Ozzy slowed down so he could talk to me.

"What's going on that people keep hitting on you tonight?" Ozzy asked. "Does that happen to you all the time?"

"No, and it didn't happen tonight. He just knew where I got my hat. It was his cousin's dad or something. His cousin's brother—I'm not sure. This Josh guy who made this. He's related to Colton."

"How do you know so much about Colton McManus?"

"I don't. Just the hat thing and that his sister is my vice principal," I said. "And he wasn't hitting on me. Neither was Sam."

"Both of them were, but I'm glad you don't care enough to notice," Ozzy said.

By this time, we had made it to his family. They were waiting on us to say goodbye, and I set down my glass of water so that I could hug about eight people who were leaving. Our little section cleared out some, but there were still a lot of people in the crowd, so we condensed, freeing up two tables to let a different group take them over.

Ozzy kept me near him the whole time we watched the second half of the show. He didn't always make contact obvious, but he would make sure I was close and I often felt his hand touch me. His skin on mine affected me like I had never been affected before.

One other time, he saw something and took off to photograph it, leaving me alone for a minute. And when he came back, he checked on me and apologized.

"I want you to do that," I said to him. "I like watching you work. It's amazing to see it in your expression when something speaks to you. I tell myself—oh, he's getting ready to take off."

Ozzy came around and stood behind me, smiling as he spoke near my ear. "I miss you already," he said. "I never have trouble leaving Galveston, Evie. You're giving me so much trouble."

I grinned and pulled back just far enough to focus on him. His family was all around us, so I pretended to be more casual than I felt. I desperately wanted him to stay in Galveston and never leave, but all I said was, "I miss you already, too."

I had a conversation with Billy Castro before we left the venue that night. Ozzy told him I had a good jab, and Mr. Castro invited me to participate in a beginner's boxing class at the gym. I agreed that I would call the gym and set up a time so he could make sure to be there when I came to it. He was a legendary boxer, and yet he actually seemed excited about meeting me at a beginner class, which was crazy.

I was thinking about it several hours later when Ozzy dropped me off at home and he and I were squeezing every last moment out of the evening.

"What if I get good at boxing by the next time I see you?" I asked.

"Are you seriously going to start?" he asked.

"Yes," I said. "I need gloves and stuff, though. Could you put together a shopping cart for me so I know what to get? And what clothes and shoes do I wear when I go there?"

"At our gym, you wear just regular athletic clothes, and we go barefoot. Most people wear sandals or tennis shoes in and then take them off when they go on the mat. But maybe Uncle Billy's gym still wears tennis shoes at boxing class. I'm not positive. He'll tell you what you need. Just wear athletic stuff. It's lowkey."

"You're lowkey," I returned.

"Maybe on the outside," he said. "But over here on the inside, I'm thinking about all the dudes at that gym who I'm about to have to fight if I hear about them looking at you."

I laughed like he was joking, but I secretly hoped he wasn't.

CHAPTER 14

Ozzy

Boston, MA
Four months later

October

*O*zzy had been in Boston working for the last two weeks. He made a few connections in the music and film industry, and those relationships led to a job as the director of photography in a short film/music video by Tom Waits. Ozzy's mom had always been a fan, and she introduced her boys to his music when they were young. Ozzy jumped at the chance to work with Tom.

Production happened in Boston, mostly in an old Catholic church, but also some at a restaurant and there was a scene in someone's personal residence.

Ozzy had been on location for two weeks. They worked on the project most days, but when he had some time off, he would tour around New England and take drives to the country to look at the fall colors.

He didn't get to this part of the country much and it was a beautiful time of year, so he used the opportunity to do some sightseeing and some outdoor photography. Ozzy still kept in touch with his professor from college. He was from Boston and he told Ozzy about all the best outdoor places for photos.

Ozzy tried all of them, and today, he worked in one of his favorites from the bunch. It was an industrial area with some graffiti and trains. He took photographs of Graham Jackson there. Graham was the unusually tall center for the Boston Celtics. All NBA centers were tall, but Graham was an oddity.

Ozzy had been the one to contact Graham. Graham was an up-and-coming basketball player who was seven feet four inches tall with a really interesting build and face.

Ozzy was now officially finished with the music video, and he contacted Graham via social media to set up a shoot while he was still in Boston.

Graham met him in the industrial part of town. He was an interesting looking human being, and Ozzy went into artist mode for an hour with Graham. They wrapped up, and everything was great. He got some amazing shots that he knew Graham would love.

Ozzy was in a great mood. He stopped in a convenience store on his way back to his hotel. He went inside to get a few bottles of water, and he was hungry enough to peruse the snack aisle.

He stared at a pack of BBQ-flavored Corn Nuts, trying to remember whether or not he liked that snack. He looked over a few other things like Combos and Cheese-its.

He was staring blankly at the selection of various salty snacks when his whole world changed.

Suddenly, and out of nowhere, he heard loud yelling, and then a shriek, and then the loud popping sound of gunfire. It was so loud that Ozzy ducked and covered and barely registered the continued shrieks that came after it.

Someone fell down in the aisle in front of Ozzy and then proceeded to scramble and shove Ozzy so desperately that it hurt. It was a middle-aged gentleman who was dressed like he had an office job. He scratched and crawled frantically, scurrying clumsily to get behind Ozzy, to push Ozzy in front of him.

Ozzy resisted him as much as necessary, but he remained calm, listening, peering carefully toward the register. He inched forward, looking around the corner to see what was going on.

"GET UP! Get up and open the register right now!" The man was waving a pistol, pointing it violently behind the counter.

Ozzy assessed the situation. Two people were down on the floor between himself and the guy. They were huddled together and hugging the wall. The guy was focused behind the register, but then he turned to someone else who was on the floor to his left. "Stop it, STOP IT!" He faced the cashier, pumping his arm to threaten her again with the gun. "Calm down! Get up! Stop crying!"

Ozzy heard wailing from behind the register and then more yelling from the guy with the gun. Then the guy turned and started yelling at someone to his left again. He was saying something about videoing and he threatened that person and pointed the gun down at them, which made them shriek. It was a lady. The guy turned to the register again and yelled something about getting the money. In frustration, he lifted his pistol, and fired another shot into the air, causing glass to shatter and people to cry aloud again.

A year ago, there was simply no way Ozzy would try to be a hero in this situation. He wouldn't even think about it. He might try to fight injustice with photographs or even words, but physically, Ozzy was not prepared for an altercation.

Now, however, he was very prepared. For nearly a year, he had trained his body in difficult physical situations and he was a different man than he used to be because of it.

Glass was broken, people were crying, the man with the gun was losing his mind, and Ozzy sprang into action. He stood up running and took three leaping strides toward the man's back before tackling him and taking him down. They both fell to the floor, and Ozzy held on for dear life and rolled over with him twice.

A shot got fired in the scramble, but Ozzy stuck to the plan. He controlled the guy, latching onto his back and wrapping his arms and legs around his mid-section so he had no space and could not get away.

Ozzy tightened his legs and arms around the man's torso, holding him securely in place in front of him. He held on tightly, burying his face in the guy's upper back and neck so that he couldn't turn around. Ozzy wrapped his arms around the man's neck in a very practiced sequence of moves that only took seconds. He knew the most efficient way to get into position and just the right muscles to contract once he got there.

Within a minute, the man went from fighting, to flailing, to still. He stopped resisting and his body went limp and unconscious. Ozzy held him there for another second. There was still yelling and crying.

"I've got him down!" Ozzy announced in his calmest but loudest tone. "Everything's fine. I've got him here, but I need someone to call the cops."

Ozzy let go of the choke and grabbed the gun, but he knew they didn't have much time before the guy woke up and started fighting again, so he repositioned him face down, holding his arms behind his back.

"I already called the cops," a woman announced.

"The cops are coming, I can hear them," someone else said.

The next several minutes were surreal.

First, Ozzy had to manage the guy waking up. He was fighting but he was weak, dazed, and mad—flailing and cursing constantly. He scrambled violently, but Ozzy had control of the gun, therefore he ultimately controlled the guy. Ozzy had to yell impassively at him to get him to stay put.

"You've been shot," someone said.

Ozzy vaguely knew the lady was talking to him. He looked at his own arm, and saw that there was blood and a gunshot wound. Just the sight of it made him feel woozy.

He was in Boston.

He had to keep it together.

He had to get home.

Ozzy thought of home, and his mind went to Galveston.

Home was Seattle.

He needed to get to Seattle.

But it was the thought of Galveston that kept him focused. Evie.

Those minutes were all about prioritizing.

The cops came and Ozzy kept it together enough to tell them what they needed to know. He spoke quickly enough that they knew he needed medical attention. One of them knew how to make a tourniquet for Ozzy's arm, and they worked on that while the other one arrested the criminal and began speaking to the witnesses.

The guy was in the back of the police car by the time Ozzy got taken away by the ambulance.

They had to do surgery to remove the bullet, which was still in Ozzy's arm when he got to the hospital.

Ozzy remembered the scramble, and he put it together that the bullet might have ricocheted off the floor before hitting his arm. The doctors agreed that it was a more likely scenario since it hadn't gone all the way through.

Ozzy called his mom before he went into surgery.

"Hey," he said. "I have to have a little procedure here in Boston."

"What procedure?"

"Just listen, Mom. I finished all my work with that video, but I might miss my flight back. I wanted to tell you so that you could tell Evie for me. I don't want either of you to come up here. I'm seriously fine. I'm in my right mind. I know what's going on, and I'm in good hands. It's just a small procedure."

"Procedure for what, Ozzy? Why wouldn't you be in your right mind? Where are you? In Boston? What kind of procedure?"

"Mom. This is why I called you and not Evie. It's nothing to be nervous about. I don't want you guys freaking out and coming up here or anything."

"Ozzy what is going on?" She asked with panic in her voice.

"Mom, I'm fine. I'm sitting here on my phone, talking to you right now."

"Where are you."

"In Boston."

"Where in Boston?"

"I was in a gas station and there was a situation with the man and a gun, and it sounds a lot worse than it is, I promise. I'm in good hands. It's going to be a quick procedure and they'll bandage me up. It's just my arm. I'll probably just be in here for one night."

"Are you in a *hospital*, Ozzy?"

"Yes, Mom, but not for long."

She let out a breath and whimper, and he heard the panic in the sound of it.

"Do not come up here, Mom. I'm serious when I say I'm fine. I'm going to stay here and recover for one day, and then I'm going to Galveston straight after. I might not even tell Evie any of this happened. I don't want either of you coming up here to just turn right around and have to go home. I'm coming to Galveston in like two days."

CHAPTER 15

Evie

*I*t was a Thursday evening at 7pm when Jenny Abramson called me.

I had been in a long-distance relationship with Ozzy for months, so I had Ms. Jenny's number saved on my phone. I thought I would hear from Ozzy about an hour ago, but I was never surprised when he couldn't call me on time. That was the nature of his job. The perfect photo waited for no man, and sometimes he couldn't call exactly when he hoped he could.

He had been in Boston for two weeks, and it had been that way the whole time. It was always like that when he traveled—our phone schedule was off. We talked when we could.

I thought it would be him who was calling me that evening, but it was his mom. I smiled and didn't think anything of it when I answered the phone.

"Hey Ms. Jenny."

"Hey, sweetheart, how are you?"

"I'm fine. Busy with school. It's a busy time of year. We're going full swing before the holidays get here. How are you?"

"I'm good, baby, I'm actually calling about Ozzy. He's fine. I talked to him on the phone, and I actually just called up there and talked to his doctor as well, and he reassured me."

My heart dropped.

"What happened to Ozzy?" I asked, cutting in while she was still talking.

"There was a fight, and he got shot in the arm."

"Shot?"

"Yes," she said.

"With a gun?"

She let out a sound. I thought she was laughing, but then I realized she was crying.

"I'm sorry, baby. But he's fine, Evie. He didn't want you to worry. He'll miss his flight tomorrow. He's thinking he'll be able to check out tomorrow and fly home Saturday. That would just push his trip back one day, and he said he was coming here and not going to Seattle. He made me promise to tell you that. He's coming straight here, and he'll be here Saturday—Sunday at the latest. He said that neither of us should go all the way up to Boston to just turn around and come back."

I had so many questions, I didn't know which to ask first. "And what did the doctor say? Did he, the doctor, say it was no big deal?"

"Kind of. I mean, they hate to make any promises, but he did say several times that it was a routine procedure."

I thought of what the actual procedure was. I thought about there being a piece of metal inside of Ozzy, and I felt nauseated.

"I'm sorry, Ms. Jenny. I know he told you to make sure you told me to stay and everything, but I'm going up there. I feel like I just need to go there and be with him."

"I felt the same way. I didn't know what to do. It's hard for me to take the day off work. If Sean and I leave, we have to close the business. But I wanted to go. I told Ozzy I would book a flight out today, and he specifically asked me not to. He said it'd give him motivation to get out of there faster. And you have school. He didn't want you to miss any days. He said he's coming straight here and for us not to worry."

"I haven't missed an hour of school this whole semester," I said, resolutely. "I'll take tomorrow off. It's no big deal. I'll take Monday, if I need to. I want to be there for Ozzy. What hospital is he in?"

Jenny took a deep breath. "Oh, Evie, I'm supposed to advise you against this, I really am. But thank you, baby. Thank you, Evie. I wish you would go to him. Are you really thinking about it? It would be amazing to have you there, even just to be with him in the airport to help him get back."

"Yes," I agreed. "I'm going. What hospital?"

"He's at Tufts Medical Center. And I have the name of his hotel in my—"

"I know his hotel," I said. "Thank you. I'll look at tickets and let you know what I come up with."

***

143

My best flight option was to leave Houston at 6am, which would put me in Boston before noon the following day. I bought a one-way ticket and would try to get on whatever flight Ozzy booked to come home. I didn't care how or when I got home. All I cared about was getting to Ozzy as quickly as possible.

The evening came and went, and before I knew it, the wheels were set in motion, and I was making the trip to the northeast. They kept Ozzy overnight at the hospital, but I had been in touch with the charge nurse and I knew they had plans to discharge him today.

He called me three times when I was on the plane, so I called him back right when I landed.

"Hey," he said, sounding happy.

"Hey," I said.

"Where are you?" he asked, hearing the noise.

"Where are you?" I asked.

"I asked you first," he said.

"I'm in an airport," I said. "And for the answer as to why I'm in an airport, you should answer the question as to where *you* are."

"Are you coming to Boston?" he asked.

"I'm already in Boston," I said.

"You're joking."

"Nope. Are you still at Tufts?"

"Yes. Evie. Where are you? The airport?"

"Yes."

"How are you going to get here? I'm worried about you."

I had just stepped off of the plane, and I moved to the side, propping my luggage and my leg on an empty chair so that people behind me could pass.

"Don't worry about me," I said to Ozzy. "But I'm glad I'm talking to you. I talked to a nurse earlier who said you might be discharged today. I didn't want to go to the hospital and find out you were already gone. I was about to call again since I hadn't heard from you last night."

"I'm sorry. I didn't call because I didn't want you to drop everything and come to Boston."

"Too late," I said.

"Get over to me," he said.

"I'm trying," I replied, laughing as I started walking again. "I just landed. I'm barely off the plane, but I'm on my way. Are you okay? Are you feeling okay?"

I had already talked to his nurse, but I wanted to hear it from Ozzy.

"No, I'm fine. The doctor just came in and said everything looks good, but it'll be later before I'm ready to go. They're waiting on some bloodwork, and I just got this new bag of... you didn't have to come, Evie. I was going to come home to Galveston when I leave here."

"Well, you still can. I hope you still do," I said, walking through the airport and following signs for baggage claim. I didn't have any checked baggage but I knew that was the right way to go.

"Okay, let me concentrate," I said. "This is a big airport. I'll be fine, I just want to concentrate. I'll see you in a few minutes."

"I love you, Evie. Be careful."

"I will. I love you, too."

I had to put on my big girl pants to make it through that airport and get a cab to the hospital. I just pretended to know what I was doing, but I wasn't what you'd call a world traveler and I didn't have much practice at dealing with taxis. I figured out, too late, that I should have tried my hand at Uber, but the yellow taxi would have to do.

It smelled musky in there, and it kind of felt like I was in a cop car, but the driver was nice enough and he seemed to know where I was headed, so I just sat in the back and hoped for the best. He was really quiet. I figured he thought I might not want to talk since I was headed to a hospital.

As soon as I got to Tufts, I found out that Ozzy was in the North building on the seventh floor, but before I went to his room, I visited the restroom. I needed to use it and I didn't want that to be the first thing I had to do when I saw him. I also wanted to check myself in the mirror and scrub the day of travel off of my hands.

I packed light and only had one bag and a purse with me, so it was easy to get around. I wasted no time finishing up in the restroom so that I could make my way to Ozzy's room.

I rode up the elevator and walked down hallways in search of his room.

One lady asked if she could help me, but I thanked her and told her I knew where I was going.

I gave two knocks on Ozzy's door before cracking it open.

"Come in. Come here to meeee," I heard him say, moaning.

I rounded the corner, and I saw Ozzy sitting there. My heart ached at the sight of him sitting in a hospital bed with a tube in one arm and a bandage and sling on the other.

My face must've reflected my concern because the very first thing Ozzy said to me was, "I'm fine. I'm fine, Evie."

"This is seriously my worst nightmare ever, Ozzy." As I spoke, I found a spot nearby to set my bag and purse. I turned and went to him. I wore comfortable clothes—stretchy jeans and a Clemson sweatshirt that my brother had bought me for Christmas.

I went to the bed next to Ozzy and leaned over, coming close to him, going to him for a tentative kiss.

"Come here," he said, sounding impatient.

I was concerned for his comfort with the IV and the sling, but I was relieved to see him alive and acting like he wanted me closer. I kissed him. I could still smell his underlying scent even though he now smelled sterile, like the hospital, detergent, and soap.

I didn't want to hurt him, but I also couldn't keep my hands off of him. I held onto his face, gently touching him, feeling him, feeling ever so grateful that he was alive.

I couldn't stop myself from crying. Huge, hot tears formed in my eyes and ran down my cheeks.

"You smell like the hospital," I said, trying to change the subject so he wouldn't mention the tears.

I leaned in to kiss his cheek with such tenderness that it took me several seconds to do it. I was standing next to the bed, and he leaned toward me. He was big and handsome, and the fact that he survived a gunshot wound made him have a dangerous edge that caused my heart to pound.

I was actively crying from relief while at the same time getting all hot and bothered by the thought of his heroics and the feel of his skin under my fingertips—his very alive skin.

"I just love you," I said breathlessly, explaining the tears. But saying it made me cry even more, and my voice was high-pitched.

"Why are you crying, my love? Come here. Come sit with me. Look, let's get the nurse in here and see if we can get this out."

There was no use in me protesting. Ozzy had already pressed the button to call a nurse as he mentioned that.

"You don't need to do that," I said.

"Yes, sir?" the nurse's voice came over a little speaker that was built into the bed.

"No rush, but Roxanne said she'd take my IV out after this last bag was finished, and I just wanted to let you know that it is." He glanced up guiltily at the bag, which was *almost* empty.

"Okay, I'll let her know."

"Thanks," Ozzy said.

"It's pretty much empty," he said to me, once she disconnected.

I wiped my eyes and got myself in order while Ozzy scooted over, making room for me. "Come sit right here," he said.

"I will, but let's wait a minute. Let's wait until the nurse comes and goes."

Ozzy agreed reluctantly and I stood by the bed, holding his hand. I set his hand down on the bed and stepped back when I heard her open the door.

"Hey, is it all done?" she asked. "Oh, hello," she added when she saw me. She had a heavy Boston accent, and I smiled because it was familiar.

"Hello," I said.

"Roxanne this is Evie, my fiancée. She just got here from Texas, and now I'm itching to leave."

"I didn't know you two were getting married," Roxanne said. "I talked to Evie already. Hey there, Evie, it's good to put a name with a face."

"You too. Thanks for taking care of Ozzy."

"My pleasure. It's not every day you meet a famous photographer."

"I know, he's pretty special."

"I was hoping to get this thing off and see about getting discharged," Ozzy said, sticking to business and giving Roxanne a pleading expression.

"Okay, I know you're ready to go, but things just take longer than that around here. I get off at three, and I'll do my best to get you on your way by then, but no promises. You two just sit in here and relax, okay? Watch some TV. Don't be in such a hurry. This bag's got medicine in it, and it's not even quite finished."

CHAPTER 16

e called me his fiancée.

I thought of it several times during the next few minutes, but I never mentioned it. Roxanne left the room, and I pulled a chair so close to Ozzy's bed that I was basically sitting right next to him. He wanted me to sit next to him on the bed, but he had a bullet wound in one arm and an IV in the other, so I made him let me stay in the chair.

I did, however, take my shoes off and get comfortable. I basically leaned onto the bed with him so that he had plenty of room but we could still snuggle. The television was on, but it was muted. It was on a sports channel.

"Thank you for coming here," he said staring at me once I found a comfortable position.

I leaned up for a kiss when he said that. "You're welcome. I want to be here. I would have left last night, but there were no more flights out by the time I checked. I took the earliest flight there was."

He smiled thankfully at me.

"What happened, Ozzy? Can you please tell me about it? Did that guy just walk in and open fire? I talked to your mom about it, and she had talked to someone at the police station. They said you tackled him and held him until they could get there, but they didn't give her a ton of details."

"That's exactly what happened," he said. "I was in there when he came in to rob the register. This was... I guess, yesterday, after I worked with Graham. It feels like it was two days ago. I've seen convenience stores getting held up, but you never think it will happen to you."

"No kidding, Ozzy that's just absolutely unbelievable. I don't know what to say. Why didn't you just let him take the money and leave? I'm proud of you, but I hated that you got involved. I love it, but I also hate it. Why'd you step in?"

"I wasn't going to at first. I'm surprised, but I was actually really clearheaded in the moment. The cashier couldn't get it together enough to give him any money, and he was impatient. I chose to rush him. I watched him for a while, and I wasn't going to do anything at first, but the whole situation just felt... volatile. I felt like somebody was about to get hurt. I was in control when I rushed him, though. I had been watching him and I knew he wasn't going to be able to turn and shoot me or anyone else. I didn't think about a bullet ricocheting." Ozzy smiled. "But it turned out fine. The doctor took it out, no problem. He said there wasn't even much muscle damage."

I let out a sigh, leaning on the bed. "I feel lightheaded with you even saying that," I said. I rested my face on the side of his bed—my arms stretched over his lap as I held onto him protectively.

Ozzy laughed when I said that. "I felt lightheaded right when it happened, but I've been fine since. Everybody's been really nice over here. And I had visitors this morning."

"I see that," I said, gesturing to the flowers and balloons that were on the counter nearby. "Who brought those?"

"Two different groups of people came by—the music video people, and also a few guys from that gym I've trained at the last couple of weeks. I had called Tom, so I wasn't surprised to see the video crew show up, but the guys from the gym found out and came up here without me telling them it happened."

"Seriously? How?"

"They have several cops who train there, and one of them saw the video. He knew I did jiu jitsu in the scramble, and he showed it to Barry, the gym owner. Barry was the one who came by—him and a couple other coaches. He brought me a blue belt." Ozzy motioned to the bouquet of balloons, which were tied to a long strip of folded royal blue fabric. "I don't know if there's a rule about being promoted by a coach other than your own, but Barry said after he saw that video he couldn't let me leave town without my blue belt."

"Oh, my gosh. That's amazing, Ozzy. You've been working hard for that."

"Thank you. I know. I was really surprised he did that."

"What are you going to do when you get back home? Are you going to wear the new one, the blue one?"

"I'll probably wear the white because I don't want my coach to feel weird about it. But I'm going to tell him the story. Honestly, he'll probably give me my blue belt. I've heard a few of the guys talking about it, saying it's coming. There's a belt ceremony coming up."

"Is that where everybody gets a new belt?"

"If you deserve one," he said.

"Well you *definitely* deserve one," I said. "I think you deserve two."

He grinned. "Like two blue belts stacked on top of each other at the same time?" he asked.

"No, like two steps higher than where you are now. What's after blue?"

"Purple."

"I think you should be purple," I said even though I had no idea.

He laughed at that. "Not even close, but thank you. Even blue's kind of a stretch. It's a big deal to get promoted. I think Barry was factoring the, you know, the whole... situation or whatever."

"You mean the bravery factor?"

"Yeah, I guess. Although in the moment it didn't feel that way."

"How did it feel?"

"I don't know. Just matter of fact. Like I had a job to do and I just did it. I think God helped me, honestly, Evie. I know I've had a little jiu jitsu, but jumping at a man with a gun isn't really my level of training. Something just came over me. I feel like it was God."

"It was," I said nodding confidently.

"It had to be. I saw surveillance video this morning when the detective came to talk to me, and I couldn't believe that was me who did that."

"I want to see the video."

"I forgot to ask him for it," Ozzy said. "It was 7am when he got here. I was still sleeping. Roxanne came in, she was introducing herself to me and making a fuss over the way the nurse before her left my charts out of order. The officer was right behind her, and I was slow to wake up with all the pain medicine and everything."

"Are you sure you need to check out?" I asked. "I don't want you to be in a hurry."

"I'm only in a hurry because I'm well enough to be that way," he said. "I feel fine now that I'm up—and especially now that you're here."

He rested his head on the pillow. His dark curly hair hung in wild layers, and I reached up and ran my fingers through the area over his ear. I hadn't seen him in a month, and I was aching to be near him.

"I'm sad that it's under these conditions," I said when the thought crossed my mind. "But I'm so glad we're together, Ozzy. I was missing you, and it was going to be another month before I saw you again. I didn't want to wait till Thanksgiving."

"I can't wait that long, either," he said. "Riding in an ambulance gives you a reality check, Evie, and it made me realize that I have no reason to call Seattle home anymore. Mac and Morgan will be coming back soon, and Katie and Justin won't be that far behind them. And we can go back to Seattle to visit any time we want."

"Yeah," I said, agreeing with him since this plan sounded wonderful to me.

"I guess I'll look at buying a place," he said.

"I talked to Tara the other day. She and Mr. Trey have a unit for rent in that pink building on Market Street. She told me about it—she said it's remodeled."

"Tell them I'll take it," he said. "It'll be somewhere to stay until I find a place to buy. Can we call her right now?"

Ozzy sat up a little and I said, "Are you calling her? Do you want me to grab your phone?"

"Yeah, it's over there," he said. He motioned to a rolling tray. It was near enough to me that I easily reached out and retrieved the phone for him.

I sat in the chair next to Ozzy while he placed the call.

"Come sit by me," he said, while it was ringing.

I didn't want to protest while she was about to pick up, so I just stood up and then sat on the edge of his bed. Ozzy had one arm in a sling, so he used his free hand, his IV hand, to hold his phone.

I sat next to him, absentmindedly fiddling with his blanket while the phone rang. I could hear it, loud and clear.

"Ozzy?"

"Hey, Aunt Tara."

"Baby boy, what in the world? I saw that video of you."

I could clearly hear her on the other end.

"What video?" Ozzy asked.

"Of you in the gas station. The robbery."

"How'd you see that?" Ozzy asked, sounding surprised.

"Nick and Cody were over here when your mom called and told me what happened. They got it up on the computer. Nick said Cody was a *straight hacker*, whatever that means. I think he was joking, but either way, Ozzy. What in the world, baby? Your mom said she talked to you this morning and you're doing well, though. Is that true? Are you traveling?"

"Yes ma'am, I am. I'm in Boston. But I'm doing fine."

"Well, we've all been praying for you. I forwarded that video to your mom, and we both had a good cry on the phone. We're just... (her high-pitched voice cracked) so proud of you."

"Thank you," Ozzy said. "I'm pretty sure God helped me because I don't remember much of it, to be honest with you, Aunt Tara."

"I'm pretty sure He helped you, too baby. He's always helping all of us. And we were all so proud of you."

"Thank you so much," he said. "But, hey, I'm calling for a totally different reason."

"Oh, okay. Whatcha got?"

"That building on Market Street—the pink building. Evie heard you had an apartment for rent in there."

"Is Evie looking to rent something?"

"I am, actually," Ozzy said.

"You are? Are you moving home?"

"Yes," he said. "I'll still visit Seattle, but yes, I'm moving home."

"When?"

"Tomorrow."

"Whoa, that's awesome, Ozzy. Your mom's going to flip. Does she know? Hey, but that unit got rented like two days ago. Dang. Ooh, but I have something better for you."

"What is it?"

"Bank Street. My building. The building on the corner of 23rd."

"That's your house," Ozzy said.

"We've been spending all of our time out at the property," Tara said. "We have that land, and then I started getting animals, and by the time I tend to all the animals every day, it's hard to spend any time downtown. We're barely ever there. We use it certain weekends and during Dickens on the Strand and all that stuff, but anyway, we've mostly moved out."

"What about Bri?" Ozzy asked.

"Bri is in one of our other houses. She's happy over there. She's got a yard for her dog. And Nick is about to move to Spain for a year. He'll probably want to move into the apartment when he gets back, but if a year is long enough, you're welcome to take that place over. We'd love to have you in there."

"I would be so stoked to have that apartment for a year, Aunt Tara. You can pretty much name your price and I'll pay it."

"Aw, we'll work something out, Ozzy. But I'm not worried about it. I'm happy to have you move into it. That'll be perfect."

"When can I move in?" he asked.

"Whenever," she said. "We still have furniture in there. Do you mind if that stays?"

"No. Not at all."

"But I'll try to get most of our personal things out by tomorrow," she said.

"I'll just stay at Mom's for a week or so," Ozzy said.

"Okay, that sounds perfect," she said. "We'll have it ready for you by then. Oh, and hey, Ozzy."

"Yeah?"

"There's a special bonus to that building. I'll have to show it to you some time."

Ozzy smiled when she said that. "I know what it is, Aunt Tara."

"You do?"

"Yes."

"The room?"

"Yes," he said.

"Have you been in there?"

"Yes ma'am."

"Okay I should have figured you had, but I wasn't sure. Well, I'll show you how to use the trap door when you get here."

"Yes ma'am. Thank you."

"You're welcome. I'm happy you're coming home. Jenny's going to be so excited. Does she know?"

"I told her," Ozzy said. "But she's trying not to get her heart set on it. She thinks I'm just coming home for a trip—she keeps saying that. I cannot wait to rent that apartment, though, Aunt

Tara. Thank you. I'll look into buying my own place when I move out, so we'll work the timing out with Nick. Just tell me whenever you need me out."

"Oh, yeah, Nick's already committed to teaching English in Spain. He'll be there for at least a year."

"I'm excited about that place, Aunt Tara, thank you. You should take whatever furniture you want, but also don't feel bad about leaving some. I'll use whatever's still in there."

"Sounds great, baby. I'm so happy you're coming home. Nick and Bri, Cody, everybody's going to be so happy."

"Thanks, Aunt Tara."

"You're welcome, and talk to you soon."

They said goodbye and Ozzy looked at me with a mischievous expression—a smile that had my heart racing.

I reached up and touched his cheek. I couldn't stop myself. My fingers ached to touch him. "They already rented the apartment in the pink building," he said.

"I know. I heard the whole conversation."

"Okay good I figured you could, but I wasn't sure. I had it turned up when I was talking to Mom because she was at the office. So, you heard I'm moving into that place on Bank Street?"

"Yeah, and there's something slightly mysterious about it, a trap door, but I'm even not going to ask."

"I want you to ask," Ozzy said, with a smile. "Actually, I don't. I'm just going to show you."

CHAPTER 17

One month later

Just before Thanksgiving

I missed Ozzy so much I could hardly stand it. He had spent a week in Galveston after the incident in Boston. He stayed with his parents while he recovered, but he had trips scheduled afterward, and he left for Miami and then went to Italy. So, he was just now moving into Tara and Trey's apartment.

He had a few weeks off coming up and he had plans to make a trip to Seattle to get some things, but he wanted to spend most of his time in Galveston. We had talked about it and decided that I could go to Seattle with him when he went. He wanted to show me Mac's house and hopefully, go to one or two of Mac and Justin's football games.

All of that was wonderful and going to be a lot of fun, but I didn't care where we were. I was only thinking about Ozzy— daydreaming about when I'd get the chance to see him again.

I talked to him every day, and even saw his face on Facetime, but it was nowhere near the same as being next to him. I pretended to miss him less than I did. It had been more than three weeks since I last saw him, and I was so excited I could barely contain myself.

Ozzy got to Galveston at noon today, but I was trying to fit everything in before the Thanksgiving break, so I had to stay at work all the way up until 3pm.

I went straight over to Bank Street afterward. I had a key to Ozzy's apartment. He had me pick it up from Tara and Trey's house a few weeks ago. This week, I went shopping to buy some basic groceries and cleaning supplies for when Ozzy arrived. Tara had left some of those types of things in the house, but I bought some other things I thought he would need.

I had gone to his apartment a few times while he was out of town. Once, I went to check it out and make sure it was ready for him, which it was. The second time, it was to take supplies. The third time, which was last night, I went by to take some more perishable items like eggs and milk.

I also stopped by Tara's ballet studio while I was there. She knew I used to dance, and she asked if I'd be interested in teaching a kids' class. It was a beautiful studio, and I would have loved to hang out in there since Tara and the other instructors seemed so nice. But my life already revolved around kindergarteners, and I couldn't see myself taking on another teaching gig after an already draining day of teaching kids. I was honest with her, and she totally understood.

We talked for quite a while. Her kids were my age and we had a lot in common. Plus, she knew I was seeing Ozzy, and she asked me about that. She was excited that he was moving into the apartment and back to Galveston.

It was now 4pm, and I was finally on the path that would take me to Bank Street. This time, it wasn't to meet Tara or check on the apartment. It was to see Ozzy. Finally. I could not wait.

I was chomping at the bit because I had gotten held up after work by a parent. The student had been a real challenge this year, and the mom rarely made the effort to engage with me about it, so I felt like I needed to stay and talk to her.

I ran by my house to freshen up and get my mind right after a thought-consuming meeting with her. I took an Excedrin on my way home, and by the time I made it there and started getting dressed, it had kicked in enough for me to put on some loud pop music while I was getting ready.

It felt good to forget about the meeting with Braxton's mom and wrap my head around the fact that I would be seeing Ozzy momentarily.

***

I saw Ozzy sitting at a booth at Carson's.

I had been in touch with him and I knew where to meet him. He was sitting with one of his brothers, David, and a pretty young woman. She was sitting next to Ozzy, and she was positioned in such a way that it blocked my view of him. I only knew it was Ozzy because he had on his hat. I smiled at David as I came up to the table, but I couldn't see Ozzy until I made it all the way there. It was then that I realized that Ozzy was Alec.

Ozzy was not at the table and it was Alec who was wearing the hat.

That was a bit of a relief because the woman was sitting really close to him.

"Hey, oh hey, Alec, I thought you were Ozzy.

"Oh, yeah, the hat," Alec said. "I borrowed it because it bugs Cadence." (Cadence was a new girlfriend, obviously.)

"It doesn't bug me," she said. "I just said it makes you look like a gangster. Like a Frank Sinatra style gangster."

"I actually think that might be a compliment," he said, shaking his head at her.

"Where's Ozzy?" I asked David.

He nudged his chin to his right. "He went to the restroom."

I smiled and nodded. "Thank you, I'll go meet him."

I acknowledged Alec and Cadence with a nod, but I didn't say anything else before leaving. There was a jukebox between me and the restroom area, and I planned on going to it to fake like I was choosing some music when Ozzy walked by.

But Ozzy came out of the restroom just as I was headed that way, and he caught sight of me. He smiled at me, and we headed toward each other, intersecting in the diner, near the jukebox.

"Hey," he said, coming up to me with a smile. He stopped when he was about a foot away. He was breathtakingly handsome—tall, dark, and broad-chested.

He leaned in and gently kissed my cheek. I could tell he was trying to hold back since we were in public. It wasn't packed in there, but people were around.

"I was missing you," I said.

Understatement.

"I was missing you too. Why'd you get me all that stuff? I thanked Aunt Tara for the groceries, and she said she didn't buy any of it."

"It's just a few things," I said.

"No, it's not. It's a lot."

"Well, I'm just glad you're here," I said feeling shy.

"Aunt Tara loves you," he said.

"When did you talk to her?"

"I saw her in the ballet studio a few minutes ago. I was taking some stuff inside and she helped me make a trip upstairs. We talked for a while. That's when she showed me all the stuff you bought. Paper towels and toilet paper and everything."

I shrugged and smiled. "So romantic, I know," I said sarcastically.

"It actually seriously is," Ozzy said, moving closer to me, crowding my space.

I missed him so much that I ached to throw myself into his arms and kiss him passionately. I just stared up at him with a little smile.

"Tara said you're gonna start dancing," he said.

I shrugged. "She asked me if I wanted to teach a kids' class, and I thanked her and said, if anything, I wanted to be the student. So, she asked if I'd want to work on a ballet piece with a few other adults. She's got an idea for a few girls like me who are college-age or older and out of the regular classes but still want to dance. It won't be a big deal, just a small performance. I'm supposed to go by next week to dance with her a little bit."

"How am I supposed to handle knowing you're dancing right below my apartment?"

"Well, that just means you can see me dance any time."

"How about now?" Ozzy pulled back, looking me over patiently like he was expecting a performance. It was with the utmost fake confidence that I broke out and posed in two different quick, stiff ballet poses. It was fast and exaggerated enough that Ozzy laughed out loud.

He reached out and hugged me. "I missed you," he said.

We began walking toward the table.

"We already ate," Ozzy said as we walked. "David and Alex met me at the gym, and we worked out from one to three, so we were starving."

"I'm sorry I was running late," I said. "I got held up with one of the students."

"Braxton?" he asked, knowing he gave me trouble.

"Yes, actually. His mom came by, though, so at least I got to… you know what? Never mind. I'm just glad you're here. I've already promised myself I'd put that out of my mind."

Ozzy was smiling at me for saying that as we approached the table.

"Y'all take this side," Alec said.

He nudged Cadence to stand up and then he did as well. He leaned in front of us, taking a handful of fries off of the table before turning to speak with his mouth full.

"We're heading out," he said, wiping his hand on a nearby napkin before reaching up and putting the hat on Ozzy's head.

Ozzy didn't mind. He looked great in it, so he didn't flinch when his brother put it on his head.

"I'll come by tomorrow sometime," Alec said to Ozzy.

"Sounds good," Ozzy said, patting his brother's shoulder as they switched places.

Alec and Cadence both waved at us on their way out.

"She's nice," I said, talking about Cadence.

"She is, but don't get too used to any of them," David said. "None of them last more than a week or two."

"Are you talking about Alec's girlfriends?" I asked.

"Yeah. He was with somebody else last week."

Ozzy pulled the basket of fries over toward me and I picked up a few of them. "He's a rock star," I said. "You know what they say about women and rockstars..." I trailed off because I actually had no idea what they said.

"What do they say?" Ozzy asked, pulling back to focus on me with an amused grin.

"That... women like them, or whatever." I shrugged. "I mean, I'm more into photographers but I know a lot of girls do like rock stars."

"Ozzy is a rock star, too, he's just posing as a photographer because he makes more money than us."

"Way more," Ozzy said, messing around with his brother like they always did.

"Way more for now," David said, giving it back to him.

"I do actually believe that," Ozzy agreed. "I think one day I'll be taking pictures of you touring arenas."

"Speaking of you taking pictures, we're sending that video to some record labels. We're going to do a package with that, and a demo EP with five songs—just to see if we can get any bites."

"Let me in on the packaging," Ozzy said.

He reached for my hand under the table. I didn't say anything. I just looked at him as he spoke to his brother. I was suddenly focused on the feel of his skin on mine.

"Tell me when you get a package together and you're ready to send it out," Ozzy said. "I can't promise a record deal or anything, but I can, at least, make sure it looks good and that it'll get to someone who will listen to it—that it won't get lost in the shuffle.

"Oh, Ozzy that would be amazing," David said.

"I wish I could get you guys hooked up with a deal," Ozzy said. "I don't know anybody in the record industry well enough to ask for those kinds of favors, but I'll definitely get it into the right hands."

"You could just physically threaten somebody, Ozzy. Have you seen this boy train?" David asked, looking at me. "Uncle Billy's got a jiu jitsu instructor—some black belt guy from California. You should have seen Ozzy rolling with him. It was intense. I would have never known you just got shot in the arm."

"It was fine," Ozzy said. "We weren't trying to kill each other."

David looked at me. "Basically, my brother can kill you just by looking at you."

"I cannot," Ozzy said. "I got my butt handed to me by that guy. But I don't think I'm going to need to threaten anybody for you guys to get a record deal, anyway, David. I think you sound amazing."

"I do too," I said.

I had gone to see David and Alec's band twice while Ozzy was out of town. I was a fan, and I knew they could make it in the mainstream market.

"What can I get you, Ms. Evie" Maggie came by the table wearing a smile like always.

"Just a milkshake, please."

"In a paper cup?" she asked.

"Yes please."

"Sure thing. Chocolate?"

"Yes ma'am."

"Whipped cream and a cherry?"

"That would be great."

"No malt?"

"Yeah, go ahead with the malt, why not. Thank you, Ms. Maggie."

She smiled. "Anything else for you boys?"

"No ma'am," David said.

Maggie gave a nod and took off for the counter.

"Evie's taking a ballet class with Aunt Tara," Ozzy said to David.

"This Evie?" he asked, his eyes wide.

I nodded and smiled at David's surprise.

"I thought you said she was doing boxing."

"She is."

"I am," I agreed. "But Ms. Tara's going to see about putting together a grown-up ballet class. She mentioned some of her instructors or college-aged ex-students being interested."

"What's the action on that?" David asked, popping his knuckles.

"What?" I said.

"What do I have to do to get in on that… to be the guy who holds them up?"

David was looking at me like he was serious, so I said, "What do you mean?" I smiled at him like I was confused.

"You know, the guy ballerina who holds you all while you're doing spins and flips and stuff. I've got some upper-body strength. What's it take to get in on that?"

"Do you mean become a male dancer?" I asked. "Years of training. He wouldn't just be there to hold his partner while she does flips and stuff. He's a trained dancer."

David sat back, putting a handful of fries into his mouth. "Maybe I'll call Aunt Tara and tell her I want to become a trained dancer."

170

"Just concentrate on becoming a rock star and then you can probably hold any ballerina you want," I said. Ozzy looked at me with a playful scowl, and I smiled at him. "Not me," I clarified.

CHAPTER 18

Six months later

May

$\mathscr{I}$ had known Ozzy for a year and a half now, and we had been dating for a lot of that time. He was my man, my one and only.

I was starstruck and excited every time I saw him. The newness never went away. I experienced the very same intensity and butterflies and desire every time he left and came back. He traveled a lot, but it was so nice to have him come home to Galveston instead of Seattle between jobs.

I hung out at his apartment when he was out of town. Ozzy wanted me to. He said he wanted people to see the lights on. It worked out for me because I had become active in boxing and ballet, and both of them happened right there on Bank Street.

Ozzy's apartment had been three entire units back in the day, but they were now combined and so it was the size of a house. I had gotten into the routine of taking over one of the spare bedrooms while Ozzy was out of town.

I had my own bathroom and closet, and I basically moved in with enough stuff to be able to shower and change before and after my classes. Sometimes, I even stayed the night. I didn't stay there in that capacity when Ozzy came back into town, though.

I knew when he was coming back today, and I got my stuff out before he returned. We both set aside time for our families and jobs, but we spent all of our free time together when he was at home, and I couldn't wait to see him.

I had been going to kickboxing classes two times a week. I loved getting better and seeing how impressed Ozzy was every time he came home and we did a boxing class together. So, I had been hard at work doing boxing and ballet (which oddly enough had overlapping concepts).

I didn't talk to Ozzy about ballet, though. He knew I was still working with Tara, and he checked in with me to make sure I was enjoying it, but I never showed him anything or told him details. I liked the thought of surprising him with it.

I had always liked to work hard, but Ozzy was an inspiration, honestly. He was always hustling. He was active on his own social media accounts, but he never just sat there and surfed the internet mindlessly. Ozzy lived in the moment, and he made the most of his day. If he wasn't taking pictures he was editing them, and if he wasn't editing them he was thinking of something new to do or practicing MMA.

He was a non-stop kind of guy, and I never dreamed that someone like Ozzy would be my boyfriend. It was surreal, honestly. But I didn't let on that I thought he was too cool for me. I just did my best to be cool enough to deserve him. That was why I got my booty dressed in stretchy pants, a sports bra, and T-shirt and went to Bank Street Boxing even on days when I really didn't feel like it. I worked hard when Ozzy was away because he always had stories to tell and checked up on me and my endeavors when he came home.

He had been in New York for the last ten days, and during that time, a lot had happened. I had finished up with my school year of teaching and Bank Street Ballet Company already held two out of three performances of Tara's dance.

It was the thirty-minute ballet she had choreographed for the class I was taking. Tara even had a part in it. It was about the hurricane of 1900, and it told the story. It was beautiful and thought-provoking, and I was honored to be a part of it.

The mayor had caught wind of it and come to one of our rehearsals. We had planned to do the one and only performance of it with the children's recital on Saturday night, but the mayor asked if we would add a Friday night showing and a Saturday afternoon, making three performances total.

Tara agreed, and we all told her we would do all we could to make it extra special.

Ozzy didn't know about all this. I had intentionally kept him out of the loop. He had planned his trip around getting back for the Saturday evening performance, so we left it at that.

I was excited that there was some hype around it. It was a beautiful piece and I was happy it was well received for Tara's sake. But also, selfishly, it was cool for me to experience the excitement that surrounded it, and I knew the whole thing would surprise Ozzy since I hadn't said much about it.

I could not wait to see him. I got a text while I was at the Saturday afternoon performance saying he made it home and was at his apartment, so I went straight there.

I ran into his mom outside on the sidewalk. "Hey, Evie, I was just inside with Ozzy. He's expecting you."

"Oh, good," I said.

"Hey, I heard such good things about that show you're putting on. Sean and I have tickets to see it tonight."

"Oh good."

"Are your parents coming?" she asked.

"No ma'am. I should've invited them. Tara said we were doing it again next year if all goes as planned. I'll have to invite my mom to that."

"Okay, well, it was good seeing you," she said, giving me a loving pat on the shoulder. "I'll see you tonight."

"Yes ma'am, see you then."

"Hey Evie," she added, stopping in her tracks. I turned to look at her when she said my name. "I don't know how to say this other than to just thank you."

"For what?" I asked.

"For getting my boy back home," she said. "I don't know if he would have ever moved back here if it weren't for you, and now I feel like he's here to stay."

"Oh, well..." I trailed off, not knowing what to say.

"And he's always been a good boy, but he wants to be good for you, Evie." She smiled at me. "He just seems like he is on the right track, I think you were the one who put him there."

"Oh, I feel like he put me on the right track," I said, not knowing how to take the compliment.

She reached out and hugged me and I hugged her back.

"I'll see you tonight," she said.

"Sounds great," I said. "Thanks for coming."

"We're looking forward to it!" She spoke over her shoulder as she began to walk down the sidewalk.

The door leading to Ozzy's apartment was on the sidewalk right next to the ballet studio, and I went through it without knocking.

It was locked, but I had the key. I entered a room that had a massive wooden staircase leading to the doors of his second-story apartment. I climbed the stairs two by two because I was so excited to see Ozzy.

I went to the closest door and knocked on it without hesitation. I had on my ballet tights and my hair was in a bun, but otherwise I had changed out of my costume and into jeans and a t-shirt. I stood at his door, shifting my weight nervously from side to side as I waited for him to open it.

I didn't care that I hadn't quite caught my breath when he got there. I smiled as he smiled and he took me into his arms.

He held me and I looked up at him before he kissed me... 1,2,3,4,5 times... it didn't matter. They were quick, gentle relieved kisses that came one after another.

I never got tired of the taste of Ozzy's mouth—the feel of it. I ached to kiss him, and it made me feel alive with sensations while it was happening. I ran my fingers through his wavy black hair. The texture of the curls was like heaven on my fingers. We kissed and hugged and just stood there greeting each other in the most patient, relieved greeting you could ever imagine.

"Your hair," he said, after a while.

"Oh, yeah, you never see me in a bun," I said.

"I met you with a bun," he said. He gave me a tight, playful squeeze that made me squirm and laugh.

"I messed up on this one. I need to take it out and redo it for the last show. I was planning on doing that."

Ozzy looked me over. "It's literally perfect," he said.

I smiled. "Thank you, but it's not. It's smooth, but it needs to be about an inch higher. I didn't leave myself enough time to redo it for the first show, but I'll get it right for the second. I'll feel more confident if it's where I want it."

"Why does an inch matter? I can appreciate wanting to get pretty lines and angles, but from where I stand, I'm looking at perfection."

He looked me over and I smiled. "Well thank you, but I definitely like it higher. It's coming out."

"Take it down then," Ozzy said, not letting go of me.

"Sure," I answered.

I stayed in his arms as I reached up and began taking pins out of my hair. I had done it so many times before that I made quick work of it. I took ten or twelve pins out of my hair in as many seconds, and I unwrapped my bun and took my

BACK TO BANK STREET

ponytail out in one fluid motion. I pulled away from Ozzy just far enough to lean over to give my hair a shake. I straightened again, looking at him with my hair now wavy and full and probably looking a bit wild from being twisted into a bun.

I ran my fingers through it.

Ozzy stared at me for several long seconds, looking like he was deciding what to say. "I've had several women in my life, Evie, all for long periods of time."

CHAPTER 19

"Thanks, Ozzy, that's great. I love hearing how you've had all sorts of women."

He smiled and shook his head a little at my sarcasm. "I'm going somewhere with this, Evie. Just listen—hear me out."

We had just come into his apartment and were standing comfortably in the living room.

"What I'm saying is that before, I loved having a woman as a companion. Women are smart and funny and loyal. I would let myself get close to people, women, and only want the relationship for the companionship. I didn't want to check in with anybody, or owe an explanation to anyone, Evie. I would obviously rather lose them than commit to them in that way, because I lost them all. I liked hanging out with someone, but then I had to face it that I was basically leading them on. I had to sit there and choose a couple of times, and I just chose to let people go because I didn't want to be tied down in that way."

He paused and stared at me. His apartment was wonderful, and I loved being in there with him. I felt at home, nostalgic.

Ozzy gently pulled me in, getting closer to me. He regarded me with a serious, sincere expression.

"I want you Evie," he said in a serious tone. He ran his fingers through my hair, staring at me. "I was going to talk to you about it now that you're off for the summer and can think straight, but I would love it if you don't go back to teaching next year. Or maybe do one more year and then quit. It's up to you. It's your choice. But I make enough money for both of us. You don't have to make every single trip with me, but... I want you to be able to travel with me if you want to." He paused and licked his lips making a serious, contemplative expression as he looked at me. "And this stuff where you live here when I'm gone, and move out when I'm here—that really put me over the top today. That's backward if anything. You should be here with me when I'm in town, and when I'm gone, you can sleep at Evelyn and Carl's. I was just sitting here, complaining about that to my mom. She was here right before you left."

"I know," I said. "I ran into her on the street."

"Well, I told her all that about how I felt and how much of a bummer it was every time I had to leave you, and she thinks I should ask you to marry me."

I laughed. "She does? What do you think?"

"I think she's right."

"You do?" I asked.

He grinned at me. "Yes. I mean, you don't have to come with me on trips or quit your job for us to get married. It could stay like it is right now where you still work. But no more moving out of my house. It bums me out so hard to go in that spare bedroom and smell you in there but not see any of your stuff. It made me feel like you were here and you left."

"I was here and then left," I said.

"Yeah, that's what I'm saying. That's terrible. I'd like to be done with doing that. Can we please be done with that? I don't want you to move out when I come back anymore. I think that means we need to think about getting married. Would you marry me, Evie?"

"Yes, I would, Ozzy."

I answered in a matter-of-fact tone.

We just stared at each other.

It seemed too easy for a proposal.

"Was that you actually asking?" I asked, double-checking.

"Yes," he said. "I'm sorry. I've thought about getting a ring, and I just never have. I'm serious about this, though. If you need a ring, we can go somewhere today. If you need a grander gesture, I can do that. I didn't plan on just randomly asking you in my living room like this. I thought about different ways to propose to you. I still will do one of those things if you want me to."

I paused for a few seconds, thinking about it.

"If you did that, it might make this moment right here seem less real." I looked straight at him, staring up at him, blinking through my lashes. "Is this moment real?"

"This is as real as it gets. I'm desperate, Evie. I need you with me. I need all of you." He sounded desperate, and he leaned down, holding onto me.

I held him back. I was at least as desperate as he was.

"Yes, obviously, Ozzy," I said. "I don't need a big show for a proposal to be real. If you tell me you want to marry me, I believe you."

"Well, I'm telling you," he said.

"Okay," I said. "When?"

"Just like that?" he asked. "Just pick a date?"

"Yeah," I said. "I think that's how you do it."

"Soon, then, Evie, please. This summer. Sooner. Anytime. I'm ready when you are." He held onto me with a raw sort of tenderness that was on the brink of passion. He gripped me, touching my skin, feeling my arms and my back, running his hands over my shoulders and sides, moving slowly, holding me with expert care.

"Yes, Ozzy. A million times, yes. Let me get through this last dance tonight, and afterward later tonight, we can talk about it and pick a day."

"But we're doing it soon, you think?" he asked.

"Yes," I said, smiling at him since I could tell he was completely serious and I loved it.

"How did the shows go?" he said. "I can't believe you're doing so many."

"Sold out," I said. "That whole auditorium was packed, both shows. They talked about it on the news—on TV and in the papers."

"I didn't know it was such a big deal."

"I didn't tell you because I wanted to surprise you. Tara did an interview with your Aunt Izzy, and they showed it on TV.

It's been packed. But I made sure you got good tickets tonight. Front and center."

"I cannot wait," he said.

"I cannot wait to eat afterward," I said. I patted my own tummy. "I've been being good, trying to fit into my costume, but I'm about to tear up a chicken sandwich at Carson's after this."

He smiled. "I better take you somewhere fancier than Carson's. I thought tonight was supposed to be no big deal— that it's just part of the little kids' recital. But Mom said Uncle Josh saw it last night and said you were stunning."

"Oh, I didn't even know Uncle Josh was there," I said. "It was packed. I don't know who all was there. I didn't want to tell you because... I don't know, I just wanted you to be surprised."

I held onto him and we stood there for another twenty minutes, holding onto each other and feeling relieved to be together—kissing, talking, embracing. My fingertips were on the side of his cheek a little while later when his expression suddenly changed. He made a face like he was trying to think of something.

"Wait. Wa-w-wait. Downstairs," he said. "I think there's something downstairs that applies to us right now, Evie. Come here. Baby. Come downstairs with me." His eyes met mine. "Is anyone down there in the studio?" he asked.

I shook my head easily. "No. Everyone's at the high school for the shows. What's going on, Ozzy?"

He took me by the hand, pulling me farther into his apartment. I knew where the secret passage was, and I knew he was headed for it.

There was an entire room hidden in the wall of this place. He had to access it behind a bookshelf in the living room. It was wonderful. I had been in it several times with Ozzy. There was a skylight and a gorgeous oversized chair in the corner of a sitting area. Two walls were covered in intricately carved built-in bookshelves.

We stepped inside, and I smiled at the way it made me feel warm and fuzzy every time.

"Come on," he said, acting in a hurry.

"Where are we going?"

"You wouldn't believe me if I told you."

"Try me," I said.

"Just come with me."

Ozzy pulled me through the secret room. He crossed to the other side where we found a spiral staircase going downward.

I knew it led to a hidden door in a closet in the ballet studio. I had been through it before.

We walked down the stairs, me following him.

"Are we going into the studio?" I asked.

"Yes. There was this thing. I just remembered it. I saw it as a kid. I remember the adults talking about it, too. I think Uncle Trey's granddad or great-granddad used to live here and work downstairs. He was a jeweler. It was a jewelry store way back in the day. Anyway, that guy was a bit of an eccentric, hence the secret passageways. There were a few things other than the room. There was a whole antique hydroponic system on the roof from where he had a garden. They found it when they were remodeling. Other stuff too. Like this thing I'm going to show you. Come look at this. You're not going to believe it."

Ozzy tried the door to the studio, and when it was locked he had to pull a certain lever and then try the door again. He looked at me as the door opened.

"I completely forgot this thing existed until a few minutes ago. I remember Aunt Tara telling my parents about it when I was a little kid," he said. "They found it in the wall when they were doing construction. Down here, in the main room. I think it stays covered so Aunt Tara doesn't have to worry about the kids messing with it. Nick showed it to me when we were in high school and one of the little windows was broken."

"What in the world are you talking about, Ozzy?

"Help me get this painting down, and I'll show you."

There was a large painting in the front room, near the front desk. I had noticed it lots of times when I was here before. It was a beach scene, and I knew it had been painted by Tara's mom, Tess.

"It's on a wire," Ozzy said, pulling it back a little to peek underneath. "So lift it up a little, then out and we'll set it down against the wall behind you. It's heavy, okay, so be careful."

"What are we doing?" I said.

"It's the emergency wall, and we have an emergency," he said.

"What?" But even as I said it, we had set the painting down and I could see a section of emergency boxes that had been built into the wall. It had been hidden by the painting this whole time.

There were five of them, all lined up, small windows built into the wall—like gorgeous little safety deposit boxes with glass fronts and metal plaques above and below each one. The signs were embossed and hand-painted metal and professionally made, simply gorgeous to look at.

Above and below each window, there were words in block print.

IN CASE OF AN EMERGENCY

Those were the words written above the glass, and under each box was written whatever was in the box.

"Aunt Tara must have had it fixed because it was the cigarette that used to be broken," Ozzy said. He tapped on the small glass window, showing that it was fully intact.

There was a metal plate underneath that said CIGARETTE, and in the little enclosure, on full display, was an actual cigarette—one lone cigarette. Sun was coming in through the big windows, and I could clearly see into the box.

These windows were lined up side by side.

The next one said:

IN CASE OF AN EMERGENCY

FOLDING MONEY

I looked at the wad of old cash and then at Ozzy.
"Yeah. It's like, from the forties," he said.

Then:

GARDEN SEEDS

And there were packets of vegetable seeds inside, also vintage.
Then, in the next box, there was a bottle of Penicillin. I stared
into the window, at the antique pill bottle, wondering if
antibiotics had an expiration date. I was sure they did, but so
did the cigarette, probably, and who had ever seen dollar bills
that looked like that? Were they even still spendable?
I was thinking of these things as I moved to the last window.
There was a small box inside of the box, and the sign said:

IN CASE OF AN EMERGENCY

ENGAGEMENT

It was a little box inside.
            I looked at Ozzy. "Is that a ring?"

CHAPTER 20

"Yes," he said. "It's an *emergency engagement ring*, Evie, and we're in an emergency engagement situation. Isn't that amazing? I think it's ours."

I shook my head, staring into the little window and feeling stunned. "It's not ours, though. Somebody bought it. It's Tara's."

Ozzy thought about that, and he made a face like he hated to go against me but had to.

"I think whoever made this little emergency station had a moment exactly like this in mind. If I put this here, I know I would love for this to be the outcome. The guy was a jeweler, so I'm sure it was fun for him to make a ring and put it in there. You never know. Aunt Tara could've already gotten it out. There could be nothing in the box, or it could be a real ring or even a plastic ring. I mean, the money and pills and everything look real, but you never know. Maybe it's all fake."

"We have to break the glass to even check," I said.

He smiled. "Yeah. That's the idea. It's an emergency, after all."

I just stood there and stared at Ozzy. "What if we break it and it's real?" I said, thinking of everything that could possibly go wrong. "Then I'm going to get my heart set on keeping it, for sentimental reasons, and I won't feel good about that. We'll have to tell Ms. Tara and Mr. Trey and I'm sure they'll want to, you know, since it technically belongs to the—"

"You're thinking about it too much," Ozzy said. "We're having an engagement emergency and there happens to be a pod built into the wall in the building we're standing in. This box is here for this exact moment, Evie."

I stared at the little box. "Who in the world would've put this here?"

"Apparently, that guy was a real character. I don't know. But it seems like we're the first people since the 1940s to have an engagement emergency, so I think it's okay for us to go ahead and do it."

"I'm breaking it," I said, looking at Ozzy, warning him.

He smiled. "I was hoping you would."

The boxes were amazing. They were intricately built into the wall by the same person who had done the woodwork upstairs in the secret room. Each little window had a small vintage ball pein hammer hanging next to it. I was about 4 inches long and the cutest thing I have ever seen.

I took the hammer into my hand and nervously tapped on the glass with it. It wasn't nearly hard enough. It barely even made a tapping sound.

I glanced up at Ozzy and he smiled at me. I was still grinning as I returned my attention to the glass. It was thin, and there was no reason I shouldn't be able to break it. The little hammer was heavy, and I let it swing slightly harder than I did the first time.

Ping.

It landed on the middle of the glass but still did no damage—not even a crack.

"You can do it!" he said, teasing me.

I gave it a whack after that, and we heard the popping sound as the glass shattered into about five or ten pieces.

"Here. Watch out. Let me get this stuff out of the way," Ozzy said, seeing that the glass was in a precarious situation. He stepped in and took the lead, and I eagerly let him since I had no idea what to do.

The sheet of glass was like a cracked egg, and Ozzy went to work clearing it out of the way piece by piece. A few pieces fell as he worked, and he said, "I'll run upstairs and get my vacuum in a minute. Just be careful."

Ozzy reached in and grabbed a hold of the box. I tried to take it from him, but he kept a hold of it until I made eye contact with him.

"Evie Taylor. I love you. I can't think about you moving out of my house anymore. I want you with me all the time. I wish you would be here, at my house, waiting for me when I get back from a trip. Marrying me is what I'm talking about. I don't think I even realized that's what I wanted until today." He held up the box. "Which is why this is an actual emergency."

Ozzy kept a hold of the box. He took one step back, away from the mess, pulling me with him. He got on his knees. He knelt comfortably on both knees, looking up at me. It was so sweet that I went down there with him. He kissed me. He broke away and then smiled in between kissing me two or three times more times.

"You were supposed to stay standing up and let me propose to you."

"You already did propose, and I said 'yes'."

He kissed me again. "You did?"

"Yes!"

Ozzy readjusted and sat down on the wood floors of Tara's beautiful ballet studio. The painting was leaning against the wall and there was a tiny bit of glass, but we sat comfortably on the floor a safe distance from it. I took the box from Ozzy, staring at it like it was an ancient artifact, which it was.

It was a small, black, leather-covered box with an antique clasp. I started to open it, and Ozzy put his hand over it, causing me to look at him. "If you like this ring and want to keep it, it's yours and I'll tell Aunt Tara I will replace it and buy an exact replica if I need to. If you don't like it, just be honest and we'll get you a new one."

"I love this moment for exactly what it is. It doesn't matter what's in this box."

"I love you, Evie."

"I love you, too," I said.

I tugged upward with my fingernail on the little clasp, hoping it would open, which it did. I lifted it for a split second and peeked inside. I barely caught a glimpse of the ring before closing the box again.

"What are you doing?" he asked.

"It's beautiful," I said. "It's too beautiful."

I didn't mean to, but I started crying. There was nothing I could do. Tears just filled up in my eyes and overflowed, running down my cheeks.

"Why are you crying?"

"I don't know. It's just so beautiful. I think it's real. Ozzy, I want it so much. I just feel happy, and scared, and sad, and relieved, and excited, and all that, all at once."

"Open it," he said. "It's yours, Evie. It was put here for us. If you like it, keep it. I'll replace it with something nice—the same thing. Don't worry about that. I'll work it out with Aunt Tara. I know her, and she would want us to… Evie, baby, are they happy tears?"

"Yes," I said, opening the ring box again. It was a gorgeous vintage solitaire—a round diamond set in a square setting. There was a little design on each side, but it was simple. The whole thing was Art Deco-inspired, which I had always loved. I put it on my finger, crying like a little baby and unable to stop. I wiped at my face, going to Ozzy, hugging him.

"This is the most perfect moment I've ever ha-a-ad," I said.

Ozzy held onto me as I took a minute to stare at the ring and let it all sink in.

***

It was two hours later when we started getting ready for the final ballet performance. Ozzy and I cleaned up our mess in the studio and then went upstairs, first to the secret room and then back to his apartment. We basked in the glory of our new engagement. Both of us were in the best moods.

We sat on the couch and talked, snuggling till the last minute when I had to rush to get dressed again. Thankfully, I got my bun right on the first try. It was in the perfect position and my hair went into an easy, smooth bun which I sprayed and pinned and tucked until it was perfect. I quickly touched up my makeup and we headed to the school.

The program would start in ten minutes, but there was an hour of children and teens before we would perform Tara's piece. Ozzy was planning on watching the entire show—children and all. He had a ton of connections in Galveston, and he knew some of the little kids that would be in the recital before we did our piece. My cousin, Valerie, was one of them.

The plan was for Ozzy to come backstage with me right now so we could tell Tara about her ring, and then Ozzy would find his seat and watch the show. I was basically on my toes the whole way inside the school. I was tired from a long weekend of dancing and I had on tennis shoes, but that didn't stop me from being light on my feet and hopping around on my toes. Ozzy held my hand the whole time, the two of us probably looking like a man holding hands with a butterfly.

I knew everybody backstage, and I talked to several of them on our way to find Tara.

We finally found her backstage in the wings, talking to Ms. Emily, one of the main coaches, a lady who had been working with Tara for years.

"Well, hey, Ozzy," Tara said when she turned and saw us approaching.

Emily walked off.

"Hey, Aunt Tara, I'm sorry to interrupt."

"No, baby, I talk to Emily all the time. I'm so glad you made it to the show! Your girlfriend is a beautiful dancer."

"That's what we wanted to... Aunt Tara, Evie and I were talking this afternoon, and we found ourselves in need of a, well one thing led to another with our conversation, and we... I remembered those little emergency boxes you found in the wall downstairs. Evie and I were in a situation where we needed one of them for a—"

Tara dramatically put her hand out in the air as if telling him to stop speaking. "Ozzy, wait," she said. "Don't you make me start crying back here before the show... Ozzy... did you? Are you talking about the little *break in case of an emergency* wall downstairs, in the studio?"

"Yes ma'am, we had to—"

"W-w-w-n-no don't tell me."

"Aunt Tara," Ozzy said sincerely. He smiled sweetly. "The moment couldn't have been more perfect. I was wishing so bad that I had a ring and the thought crossed my mind, and my heart was pounding..."

Ozzy stopped talking when Tara covered her face with both hands, moving toward us without looking, crying.

"Aunt Tara, my girl fell in love with the ring that was in there, and I was hoping I could buy it from you. We can replace the old one. I'll buy one just like the old one with new glass, and—"

Tara made a crying noise. She leaned into us. "I can't take it," she said. "Don't do this to me! I'm so happy I'm about to burst right now, Ozzy." She stepped away, wiping at tears. "I-I was, just the other day, saying to Trey what a shame it was that the emergency wall was all covered up." She came to us again and hugged us, actively, crying but trying not to. "I am losing it right now, Ozzy, thinking about y'all breaking into that."

"It was seriously just God who reminded me it was there," Ozzy said.

"Oh, don't go telling me that," Tara said. "I need to get myself together here. It's my dream come true for somebody to need that and go in there and… I tried to imagine scenarios when it would, but I never dreamed it would…" She trailed off, wiping tears again. "Did you take the ring out?" she asked, unable to even look at us.

"We did, and Evie fell in love with it," Ozzy said.

I opened my hand and tentatively stuck it into her line of vision so she could see that I was currently wearing it. It fit me perfectly.

Tara caught a glimpse, and it caused her to let out another wailing sound. She was covering her face, wiping her eyes, moving around, looking like she could barely contain herself. "I can't take it, you guys. I'm about to explode with happiness over this news. Does this mean you're actually engaged?"

"I sure hope so, or I'm a thief," Ozzy said, causing Tara to laugh and reach in and hug him.

"Thank you, Aunt Tara. I'll replace it with whatever you want in there."

"You'll do no such thing," she said, smacking him on the shoulder. "I'll replace it. It's my pleasure. You have no idea how..." She trailed off looking wide-eyed like she was begging herself to stop crying. "I'm so happy for you two," she said. She looked past us at the wall, trying to keep it together. "I'm going to try to get through this night and this... watching Evie dance when I know y'all... dang it, Ozzy, I hope I can get through this performance without crying up there on that stage. Where are you sitting? You better not be in the front row. I'm not even going to be able to look at you."

"He's not in the front row," I assured her.

"I love you Ozzy, and this is wonderful, but I can't talk about it anymore because I just imagine you two and the little hamme—" she stopped talking and took a deep breath straightening her shoulders and staring at us resolutely. "I have to think about other things right now. Y'all two need to get to where you're going because I cannot look at you right now without—I love you, but go ahead and get going to your spots, and I'll deal with these little ones."

"Yeah, save crying your eyes out for after the show with everyone else," Emily said, walking by again and catching the tail end of our conversation. "You and the seniors can all go to Carson's after the show and drown your sorrows with ice cream."

"Mine are happy tears, but these two have to get going so I don't smear my makeup all over the place."

Tara physically turned us by the shoulders and ushered us out of the backstage area, pushing, patting gently on our backs. "Have y'all told Jenny?" she asked.

"No ma'am, but she'll be here in a minute. She might already be here. I'm heading out there now."

"Okay good," Tara said, patting us both on the back as a gesture of farewell. "Tell your mom and them to hang out after the show and we'll talk then."

She was still trying to keep herself together and it was cute. She scurried away without another word, and I stared up at Ozzy.

"Have fun my beautiful ballerina," he said with a little smile.

I smiled back. "I will. That went well," I added, because I was so excited about the ring.

"It did," he agreed. "I told you it would."

"You did," I said.

I popped up and kissed his cheek. "I'll see you after the show," I said.

Ozzy smiled as he grabbed me, leaning down and giving me a quick but firm kiss.

"I love you," I said.

He smiled at me. "I loved you first."

EPILOGUE

One year later

Ozzy

Aunt Tara's ballet was such a success that she put on an encore of the performance the following May.

There were four shows and all of them sold out again. Ozzy agreed to video the last two performances. He would take the footage and piece together the best shots to make a full version.

His Aunt Izzy had already interviewed a few experts regarding the record-breaking storm that hit Galveston in 1900. Ozzy had seen the footage, and he knew he could put everything together with the ballet and make an amazing, compelling piece. The ballet itself was thirty minutes long, and the interviews were interesting and thought-provoking.

Ozzy had grown up in Galveston and heard of this disaster, but he never knew some of the things that were revealed in those interviews. It was a storm without a name. People just referred to it as the Great Storm because it was back before they started naming them.

The ballet was about resilience and grit in times of tragedy, and the interviews matched that feel. The whole project was educational, interesting, and beautiful, and it didn't even officially exist yet. Ozzy still had to put everything together. But he knew he could do it.

He never set out to be a director, but he was in the right place at the right time for this project and he felt like he had been divinely placed there to make it happen. There was no question that the story needed to be told, so Ozzy had to be willing to do it. He was proud of his Aunt Tara for making a piece of art that made you feel something. Ozzy went to several rehearsals this year, so he had seen the performance about twelve times already.

It didn't matter how many times he saw it.

The sight of his wife got him all worked up every time. He appreciated God as an artist when he looked at his wife. He loved her smile. He was so mesmerized by her mouth and eyes that he had to make ways to get around them when he filmed her.

There was a patch of embroidered beadwork on her chest. It was part of the costume. Ozzy found that if he looked at that and made sure it was in frame and in focus, he could get away with filming Evie without being distracted.

Ozzy hated to miss watching her during the last performance, though. Tara had mentioned not doing it again in the following years since they now had video footage. So, Ozzy had watched his wife through the lens tonight. It took an absurd amount of concentration and determination to both watch his wife and get good footage. Ozzy was sweaty and spent afterward, but he headed backstage with a huge grin on his face.

The performance was amazing and he was excited for Tara and Evie. He also got good footage in spite of his concentration issues, so he was happy with himself for that. He knew in his heart that it was going to be a great film. He could see it laid out in his mind before it even existed.

Ozzy walked backstage after the final performance, feeling like he was floating on air. The whole scene backstage was a lot less chaotic this year since it was not connected to a children's recital.

Ozzy had two other people filming footage of the performance, but he didn't check in with either of them. He still had a camera in his hand while he went backstage looking for his wife.

He gave a quiet whistle when he saw her because he was desperate to get her attention. She was a living work of art, and it was even better that she was dressed in her ballerina gear. Ozzy had barely kept his excitement in check the whole time he was filming, so now that he could have her, he felt that it was impossible to wait or be discreet.

Thankfully, he didn't have to do either of those things. Evie turned and grinned when she heard his whistle, and she instantly began heading toward him.

She didn't stop until she made her way into his arms. Ozzy held his camera in one hand as he wrapped himself around her, holding her tightly, never wanting to let her go.

She was officially done with school. She had committed to teaching another year at Crestview, but she was done with it now and was not going back to teaching next year.

Evie wouldn't go on every trip with Ozzy, but she would now have the option to go. And she was helping with Ozzy's local studio that they just opened. It was at their home and by appointment only, and Evie loved making picturesque scenes at their home for Ozzy to use. She would also take on a ballet class of kindergartners now that she wasn't in the classroom full-time anymore.

Ozzy could not think about any of these things, honestly. Any plans beyond this evening were distant to him.

He held onto his wife, feeling impatient to get home and do husband and wife things. She smiled and touched his forehead before touching hers. "Ooh, you're sweaty just like me," she said.

"You have no idea," he said. "I just worked harder than I ever have in my whole life. I was trying to enjoy the performance *and* film it."

She pulled back and looked at him with an expression of surprise and maybe even fear. She touched her own chest. "You didn't look at my costume?" she asked.

"No. I stared straight at your face the whole time," he said.

"Ozzy!" she said. She was straight-faced but getting onto him in a lighthearted way that told him she loved it.

"I know. So now you understand why I'm ready to get you home," he said.

"Why, so we can start editing the video?" she whispered the words near his ear, and he flexed his hands, pulling her in by the waist.

"Yep," he said. "I've got some really important editing to do."

She smiled at him. Both of them were already flush from exertion and looking at each other like they knew exactly what was about to happen.

"Thank y'all both so much!" Tara said coming up to them. She looked back and forth from Evie to Ozzy, innocently smiling and having no idea that the tension was thick between them.

"Thank you," Evie said, leaning in to hug Tara. "I had so much fun. And if I don't see her, tell Ms. Emily she did a beautiful job with the set."

"I will," Tara said. "Are you coming to eat with us? Will and Anne Rose were in the audience, and they're treating us to dinner at Elliot's."

Evie sighed. "That sounds fun. Tell them thank you. But Ozzy's all excited about the video. He's already talking about getting home to start editing."

"Yeah, I'm ready to get to work," he said. He reached in and hugged Tara. "But have fun, and tell Uncle Will we said thanks for the offer."

"I'll do better than that," Tara said. "I'll order you some dinner and drop it off at your house when I leave Elliot's. I won't bother y'all while you're editing, but I'll leave some food on the front porch. It will be nine or nine-thirty. Does that sound good?"

Nick was back from Spain and had moved into the apartment on Bank street. Ozzy and Evie bought a home with a detached shop that they transformed into his studio. Their place wasn't far from Elliot's, so it wasn't surprising when Tara offered to drop by.

"Food at nine or nine-thirty sounds amazing, Aunt Tara. Thank you. Love you. Tell everybody we missed them." Ozzy was so anxious to leave that he began pulling Evie while he was talking.

"I will," Tara said. "Thank you for dancing your heart out, Evie, and you, Ozzy, thank you for making the video."

"You're welcome," he said, walking and smiling and talking at the same time. "Congratulations, on the show, Aunt Tara. It came out great."

"All right, y'all have fun editing."

Ozzy and Evie grabbed their bags and said goodbye to about three other groups of people, including Ozzy's film crew and others from Evie's family.

"We're going to have to do some *actual* editing after telling twenty people that just now," Ozzy said.

"Oh, I thought we were editing," Evie said, pretending not to know what was going on.

They were in Ozzy's truck, stopped at a stop sign, and he stared at her from the driver's seat with an expression that was so dangerous it made her let out a laugh. He reached out and put his hand on her leg, staring at her. There was such intensity in their stares that Evie bit her lip nervously.

"Yeah," she said breathlessly. "Maybe we should do a little actual editing tonight, since that's what we told everybody. You know… later."

Ozzy cut his eyes at her, grinning as he drove. "Yeah, maybe later," he said.

The End

A few post-epilogue notes:

Back in the sixties, Billy Castro found his life's calling and
the love of his life during the same summer. Those two things
would change the trajectory of his existence. He went from a
path of crime and obligation to a life of family and God and
hope.
Professional boxing was a gift to Billy. He was able to work
hard and make an honest living doing what he was created
to do—be a warrior. Tess had an affinity for drawing and
painting beach scenes of their beautiful island home. She
worked hard, and eventually, she made a name for herself
locally and even regionally as a painter.
Billy married Tess, and they had a daughter, Tara, and a son,
Will.

Tara Castro found love in a secret room with the building's
owner. They lived upstairs, above her ballet studio for years
before buying some property where they now had a menagerie
of animals such as twelve chickens, three English mastiffs, a
pot belly pig, and a cockatoo.
Tara and Trey had two children, Nick, who spoke fluent
Spanish and spent a year in Spain, and Bri, who lived with
their cousin Mac and went to college in Washington.

Will Castro married Anne Rose Kennedy. Theirs was the
Romeo and Juliet romance, and it still felt wonderfully
forbidden, even after all these years. Anne Rose was still

a bit of a mystery to Will, and he loved that about her. He worked long hours at a family business doing a job he loved, and Anne Rose did the same. She still cooked at her family's restaurant, and all of her new recipes were just attempts to keep surprising her husband. He was her inspiration. Will and Anne Rose had two children, Cody and Caroline Castro.

Billy and Tess had two children Tara and Will, and four grandchildren, Nick, Bri, Cody, and Caroline.

***

Daniel King served in the military and then married his hometown dream-girl crush, Abigail "Abby" Cohen (Tess's sister). Daniel and Abby were an inseparable couple. Daniel took over his dad's hardware store, and Abby worked as an elementary school teacher before she quit to raise their children and help Daniel manage the business. They adopted two children, Lucy and Philip, and Abby gave birth to a third, a boy named Evan.

Lucy King met her husband on the day he broke up with another woman. Lucy had a son out of wedlock, and her little boy, Mac, was with her on the dock that day. Drew, the senator's son, had fallen in love with them both. Lucy had a successful career as a children's book author. She released the beloved Garden City series before switching to young adult novels. Her books had been on bestseller lists and had been made into major motion pictures. Lucy's younger brother,

Phillip, passed away at 22 years of age. She often used the name Phillip as a side character in her stories, and she always made him loveable.

Lucy and Drew Klein had three children Mac (whom Drew adopted) Katie, and Andrew.

Evan King married Izzy Abbott, a girl he knew and admired in high school. She worked as a news reporter, doing pieces on local businesses and people. Evan worked with Will and they built the online branch of King's Hardware into a multi-million-dollar business. They opened a factory on the south side of Houston that produced in-house hardware. Even now that they had hired hundreds of people and the business was running, Evan and his cousin spent long hours at work. They were on top of all the trends, and Kings Hardware was unbelievably successful under their leadership.

Evan and Izzy King had two children Samuel "Sam" and Audrey King.

Daniel and Abby King had three children Lucy, Phillip, and Evan, and five grandchildren Mac, Katie, Andrew, Samuel, and Audrey.

***

Laney King and James Graham met because Laney's brother, Daniel, was in the military with James. James was in a position where he had to stand up for Laney's honor, and he stepped up to the challenge. James was as solid as they came, a career

Army guy. He worked as a strategist and consultant for the Army, and he made regular trips back to Fort Benning Georgia. Laney loved being a homemaker and a mother and she gave her all to raising their twins, Jenny and Josh.

Josh Graham married a beautiful, wholesome woman named Pamela, and they had two children, Thomas and Grace Graham. Josh and Pamela had an accounting business and they ran a tight ship. James and Grace were great kids and excelled at things like winning spelling bees and science fairs.

Jenny Graham married Sean Abramson, and they had three boys who all three turned out to be charismatic and artistic. Jenny was cute and spunky, and her husband, Sean, was tall, smart, and handsome. Ozzy, David, and Alec all turned out to be handsome, talented, artistic, and funny.

Laney and James Graham had two children, Jenny and Josh, and five grandchildren James, Grace, Ozzy, David, and Alec.

***

The Castros, Kings, and Grahams had built lives and families in this charming island community. They had heartbreaks and triumphs in life, just like everybody else, but they appreciated every day and they got through the heartbreaks together. As a group, they had been given many talents. There were entrepreneurs, athletes, and artists. They stuck together and they flourished in their endeavors and in life.

But what made them special was that they knew exactly where their help came from.

Psalm 121

Thank you so much for reading the Bank Street Stories series! Goodness, I can't believe it's over.
I am truly grateful for you, my readers.
Thank you.

Also, I found that I couldn't quite let go of these characters—not after Split Decision became one of the biggest rock bands in the world.
So, the 2-part spinoff How to Tame a Heartbreaker series is now available
Hugs and blessings,
~ Brooke

Thanks to my team ~ Chris, Coda, Jan, Glenda, Yvette, and Pete

Printed in the USA
CPSIA information can be obtained
at www.ICGtesting.com
LVHW031130090224
771151LV00016B/198